The Long Night Watch

The Long Night Watch

Ivan Southall

Farrar Straus Giroux

New York

Copyright © 1983 by Ivan Southall
All rights reserved
Library of Congress catalog number: 83-48702
First published in England by Methuen, 1983
First American edition, 1984
Second Printing, 1986
Printed in Great Britain

To Susan

Foreword

The night sky began to glow, strangely so, low on the
horizon far out to sea, though nothing was there to burn of
which anything was known.

These were nights when seamen sailed without lights
and avoided collision by guess or by God, and no man on
deck put a match to his pipe if he wished to reach port
again, alive, ship-shape, and sound.

These were nights under the moon when every feather
of foam sighted by the watch was at its best a bad fright
and at its worst a torpedo on course about to strike
home.

Lights were out the whole world round; it was the Dark
Age of modern times; a light shown was a foolish or
traitorous act or evidence of a battle already being waged.

Light foretold a violent death for all concerned,
whether one sailed the seas or precariously flew or moved
on dry land, yet there the glow began to form, far out to
sea, defying all the rules. There it broke into parts and
became separate lights, a score or more, two score, four
score perhaps, becoming more and more numerous, lights
of a kind rarely seen in the history of the world – as far as
human knowledge can go with certainty, or science and
religion agree could have occurred at all.

At first, no one on the cliff-top saw the coming of the
lights. The sentry posted for the purpose was asleep, his
head between his knees.

It was 5.28 a.m. local time, about half-an-hour short of
dawn, on February 16, 1942, in the third year of the

Second World War; two months after Pearl Harbor; eight months after Hitler had headed out into Russia.

The event occurred close to the Equator at 146 degrees 50 minutes East.

In similar words I began an earlier work centred on the subject of this book – S.W.O.R.D., the Society for World Order under Divine Rule – publication of which was forbidden by Court Order after the War departments and Intelligence Agencies of several countries had become involved.

S.W.O.R.D. was founded in Melbourne, Australia, in 1936, by Brigadier Matthew Palmer D.S.O., M.C., M.L.A. In the early years of the war the Society commanded public support and provoked some anxious opposition, yet Palmer won the approval of the Australian Government of the day to undertake the remarkable expedition into the Pacific code-named Operation Sword. Successive Australian Governments have gone to lengths to conceal the fact of the expedition and to secrete or destroy records relating to it.

I refused to spell out my sources for that earlier work, believing it to be my right and responsibility. It appears, at present, that this new manuscript has made my reasons more generally acceptable. *The Long Night Watch* may well get into print, even though my home was broken into while I was writing it, the burglar alarm failing to function. I suspect that the intruder used refined methods of entry. Filing cabinets were disturbed.

The earlier work attracted comments like 'ridiculous', 'unscrupulous', and apparently grew, its critics said, from the imaginings of a deluded person.

One rash friend claimed in a letter that secret papers locked in a strong-room in Victoria Barracks, Melbourne, would prove my story. He later swore the letter was a forgery, for he had no knowledge of any such papers, that the term 'secret papers' was melodramatic, and had not the respected writers of the official history of the Second World War long ago dismissed the S.W.O.R.D. establish-

8

ment on Tangu Tangu as a 'mission station' and recorded that it was overrun by Japanese forces on or about February 16, 1942?

Professor Julius Mesek, specialty reader for Amalgamated Book Publishers, London, suggested that the story might have come to me by word of mouth from several sources. This would be consistent with instances of a similar kind of which record has survived since ancient times, the Bible being the obvious example. Contradictions were thus explained without accusing me of fraud. But if this particular account of S.W.O.R.D. were to be taken as true, Mesek went on, I was obliged to say where my material came from. The subject matter was so extraordinary that serious proof had to be supplied.

This was an odd position for Mesek to adopt in the light of his allusion to the Bible. Millions of human beings since remote times have lived by great religions founded upon writings or traditions that no one will ever be able to prove or disprove. Millions have so vigorously believed in these writings or traditions of remarkable events, that they have persecuted, imprisoned, tortured or killed millions who have not shared their beliefs.

My sources, said Mesek, had to be made public and an acceptable reason given to explain the silence of so many years. Where was my material hidden between 1942 and the present time? If I refused to answer, no publishing house could take the risk of defying the Court and incurring the hostility of the Intelligence agencies of the U.S., British, and Australian governments, and embarrassing the Japanese who appeared to have played a crucial role in the cover-up.

It is my opinion that my sources were not misleadingly concealed and the reason for the long silence was obvious.

Complement of Operation Sword

The following alphabetical list names the forty principal persons or family groups chosen to make up the original complement of Operation Sword.

Albert Edward Chambers. Born February 14, 1869. Carpenter. With two family members.

Richard Percival Cunningham, M.B.E. Born April 9, 1899. Cricketer. With four family members.

James Arthur Everard. Born August 3, 1872. Retired. With three family members.

David John Griffiths. Born November 8, 1894. Clerk. With three family members.

Jon David Griffiths. Son of above. Born March 15, 1924. Secondary student.

Hogan Hanley Hancock. Son of Jack. Born June 4, 1925. Secondary student.

Jack Hancock. Born May 25, 1904. Sheet metal worker. With three family members.

Jeffrey William Hawkins, D.F.C. Born February 26, 1896. Company director. With four family members.

Donald Gordon McBride, B.E. Born May 15, 1907. Engineer. With four family members.

Jessie Nola MacWhorter. Born July 11, 1926, at 6.15 a.m. Secondary student.

Phoebe Alison MacWhorter. Born July 11, 1926, at 4.30 a.m. Secondary student.

Virginia MacWhorter (née Higgs). Born March 3, 1901. Dressmaker.

Malcolm Bruce Oliver. Born April 28, 1917. Cabinet maker. With two family members.

Brigadier Hon. Matthew Palmer, D.S.O., M.C., M.L.A. Born January 25, 1892. Member of Parliament.

Kerry Coventry Shuffle. Born March 12, 1925. Secondary student.

Victoria Alexandra Shuffle (née Coventry), B.A., Dip. Ed. Born August 26, 1903. Former school teacher.

Henry Charles Weatheral, M.D. Born October 4, 1908. Medical practitioner. With his wife, *Vera Gertrude*, a nursing sister.

Sixty additional persons were chosen to increase the complement to a hundred souls. Detailed record has been lost. Family names, where known, are as follows:

Attwell,
Blundell,
Browning (or Brownley),
Davenport,
M. R. Douglass,
Dunne (or Donne),
Fitzgerald,
Flood,
Kingsbury (probably a U.S. citizen),
Lindsey (or Lindsay),
Rebecca Littlejohn and Martha Littlejohn,
McCallum,
Donald and Mary McCusker,
Pennyfeather,
Ramsey (or Ramsay),
Smith,
Hugh Tregellas. Born c. 1896. With his nephew
    Alan Ridley. Born 1934.
Williams.

All persons, one hundred men, women and children, went missing following an action occurring on February 16, 1942.

On December 1, 1949, the War Graves Commission posted all persons 'Missing. Believed Dead'.

Only hearsay evidence of the vaguest kind came out of the War Crimes Trials. In the opinion of the Court the Japanese action did not appear to have contravened the rules of warfare.

One

April 23, 1873 — October 14, 1941

Jon David Griffiths was the sentry on the cliff-top at
Tangu Tangu – if sentry was the term for a mere lad who
was not breaking any rules if he squatted Indian fashion
or leant on his elbow, or was allowed to make up in his
head as many words as he could out of *Hitler* or *Hammer* or
Holocaust, or was permitted to remain awake by counting
the stars within a radius of eight degrees of one major
point or another.

His guide to eight degrees was the span of sky visible
across the knuckles of his clenched fist.

'But spread your knuckles,' the Brigadier instructed
him. 'Your hand looks narrow in the beam to me.'

Spread the knuckles? How did you go about that? No
way that Jon knew of, except by cribbing with a crook of
his little finger and turning it into a six-fingered hand!

On some nights he took his count of stars up to
hundreds before he lost his way. Getting to three hundred
and twenty-six stars, one planet and three meteors, then
losing sight of your spot in the sky was like dropping the
egg the hen had taken all day to lay.

As a sentry, Jon Griffiths soon became aware of his
weaknesses, for he was armed only with his eyes and his
oath to remain awake. Not a weapon was at hand. Not a
rifle could he reach in under two-thirds of a mile. He
wouldn't have been sure how to handle a man-sized
weapon, anyway, except that with rifles you pulled the
trigger and with grenades you pulled the pin and with
bayonets you gritted your teeth and ran them in. For the

time being knowing that was enough. Plenty of opportunity later to learn the martial arts if he had need of them.

In the meantime, he was on the cliff at Tangu Tangu to raise the alarm if the invaders came in. He was up there to sound the gong, rapid blows of the mallet into the body of the long cylindrical drum, perhaps to complete an ironic circle of history.

Seventy years before, the drum had called the people of Tangu Tangu to the defence of their island as the first Christians rowed ashore with Bibles and guns. Five islanders died by the bullet that day, by the panic order of the ship's captain, and the Reverend Josiah Jones, his wife Florence, their seven-year-old son Enoch Paul, and two seamen, Phillip Fox and Tom Ready, were slain in reprisal and eaten.

Before the beginning of the Brigadier's wartime mission to Tangu Tangu, before the ship bearing its interesting passengers ever set out, the man himself began writing in the book. 'The Doomsday Book', the Brigadier called it. Jon and the others used to be curious about what it was that he wrote. He kept his eyes down most of the time, and that was good, because his eyes cut through young persons and disconcerted them. There he sat at his table on deck.

'Name?' he had demanded, not looking up at Jon, for he knew without asking.

'Jon David Griffiths. Sir!'

'David, eh? I like that.'

Jon responded with clipped words and a clicking of his heels. The click made him feel like a man. The air the whole world round was contaminated by the same disease. It originated in the Chancellery in Berlin and spread like the plague.

The Brigadier went on. 'Birth-date?'

'March 15, 1924. Sir!'

'Height?'

'Five feet eleven and three-quarter inches. Sir!' Jon didn't add that to reach the height he had to stretch so

14

much his spine felt as if it might start separating.

'Weight in pounds, stripped?'

The girls weren't in hearing, or Jon would have blushed. He did some swift mental arithmetic.

'A hundred and thirty. Sir!'

'Too thin, boy.'

'Healthy. Sir!'

'Much too thin, Jon David. Ten bananas a day, each washed down with two cups of water. Puts the weight on like the very devil.'

'Sir!'

'And take a course of *Excelsior*. Charles J. Heracles. Guarantees to add inches of muscle all round. Get onto it before we sail. Ten minutes a day, if his advertisements are to be believed, and I don't see why they shouldn't be. You must be fit. You must be strong. I have special work for you.'

'Sir!'

'Hair fair,' the Brigadier said, writing all the time, not looking up, because he knew. 'Eyes brown. Complexion sallow. Well, let's call it tan. Scars?'

'Upper left shin. Sir!'

'From what cause, boy?'

'From falling off my bike, sir, then out of the tree, when I was twelve.'

The Brigadier's eyebrows curved. His pen missed half a stroke. 'What form at school?'

'Fifth. Sir!'

'Keep up your studies. Don't regard this expedition as an excuse from other essential matters. If you're to be God's servant you give Him your best, and you'll be leaving us, of course, when you turn eighteen, to serve King and Country. You'll be sent back home to train as an officer. Be prepared for that. Tell me about your languages?'

'French, sir, five years, and two years of Latin.'

'What about German?'

'*Donner und blitzen und schweinhund und sauerkraut*. Sir!'

'To serious questions, Jon David, I demand serious

replies!'

'I have no German. Sir!'

The Brigadier looked up and his eyes cut through into the soft core, as the boy had known they would.

'Tell me, what do you hope to get out of life?'

The question took his wind away.

He wanted to stay alive.

He wanted a girl to stay alive along with him, Kerry Shuffle particularly.

'I don't want to die too soon, sir.'

It was out before he could stop it, and he regretted it. His deep flush stung his eyes and the shame welled up and he knew there'd be no special job now.

The Brigadier went back to staring at his page, his pen moving above it like a pendulum. He had a bald patch on top of his head with grey hair radiating from it. Like a monk. Or a target.

Round about gulls were crying.

'Fair enough, Jon David. . . Next!'

Hogan was next. That was Hogan, farther along the deck, looking anxious. When Hogan came up he clicked his heels also, though not as crisply. Hogan didn't have the co-ordination.

Jon wrote his letter that very afternoon to Charles J. Heracles.

Dear Mr. Heracles,

I read your advertisement in *Pix*, how you can put two inches on your biceps and four inches on your chest. Please send *Excelsior* at once. I need it urgently because of the war. As I do not know how much *Excelsior* is I cannot send you the money, but my dad promises to send you a cheque as soon as I get the bill.
Yours Truly,

Jon David Griffiths, Passenger,

C/o McPherson McBride Steamship Company,

Port of Melbourne,

Australia.

There never was a reply. The letter was conveyed to the office of the Navy censor and was there filed in a keyed cabinet marked S.W.O.R.D.

Jon wrote to his Headmaster the next evening. That letter was filed in the cabinet also, along with every other letter directed by any member of Operation Sword to any outside address.

Two

(August 14, 1932 — July 11, 1941)

To be alive then was to live on a raw edge, like the clown
Kerry saw when she was seven. There was a circus on the
vacant lot near Conlan's bakehouse and great excitement
among the kids. Kerry's father took her, holding her
hand. In those days people called him 'the man with the
little girl'. In later days they didn't remember him. He
never returned from the war.

At the circus a barefoot clown climbed a ladder of
sword-blades while Kerry sat numbed, her clutching grip
turning cold in her father's grasp. Afterwards she had
gone on living it with differing degrees of horror.

Awake or asleep, all life became part of a similar
tension, like the edge of sword-blades, Kerry stepping
from one blade to the next, no pause between them. There
were always more blades. It spoilt being young.

'We wait for a destroyer to escort us,' the Brigadier said on
deck to the assembled company of S.W.O.R.D.

For weeks the ship remained at the wharf, Navy
sentries posted, through an uneasy, nervous suspension of
familiar things. For Kerry it became another sword-blade
where she had not anticipated one would be. She had seen
the voyage as immediate, purposeful, and splendid. They
would sail away, wake foaming, horizons ahead, the
object and marvellous meaning of her life about to be
turned from dreams into real happenings.

For a few days, for the young at least, there was a discovery through every bulkhead and at the foot or top of every companion-way, but no one was allowed ashore. There were the interviews with the Brigadier, and the hourly anticipation of the voyage, and the mystery of the journey itself, and who could say what their destination would be? But everything became for young and old an anxiety, a tenseness. The food was poor. The accommodation was cramped. The ship was smelly.

They were still on the river, still at the wharf, a short but impossible leap from solid earth, and the Brigadier paced the deck like an angry Viking. Even those in his confidence began to avoid him.

Everyone ashore who cared about them thought they had gone; all the relations, all the friends, thought they had gone; though no one knew where they had gone or by what means they had travelled. They had assembled and been farewelled at the rendezvous – the football ground at Balwyn near Melbourne – then had boarded army trucks and been driven out of sight. Kerry's father believed his wife and daughter to be committed to some madness from which they'd not return alive. His despair took him to the Recruiting Office where he lied about his age and enlisted as a private soldier, while the ship was tied up less than eight miles from his silent, aching house. Had he known Kerry was still so close he may well have carried her off by force. She was only sixteen. He had the right.

On board, older people started turning cranky, started questioning their own decisions. But there were the young devotees who would have died for their Brigadier – Kerry, Jessie and Phoebe, Jon, Hogan. They were ashamed of the murmuring against the Brigadier.

'Damn fool idea,' Hogan's father said. 'How did we get talked into it? All of us committed to this rusty old tub that'll founder in the first sea or sink at the first shot!'

The Hancocks never really knew how they had become so deeply involved with S.W.O.R.D. It had happened despite themselves. Hogan felt that S.W.O.R.D. had got hold of him by the throat and dragged him into it bodily.

Not that he minded. Not really.

The ship's crew was surly. They'd been drafted from the coastal trade, didn't know what was going on and didn't like what they saw of it. There were *babies* aboard and extraordinary stores had gone into the holds. Extraordinary things. As if this were an expedition to the end of the world, as if these people were cutting themselves off from ordinary life. In wartime?

'As you know, it's a complement of a hundred souls,' the Brigadier allowed himself to explain to the ship's officers. 'Precious souls. And this the government recognizes. It's not a junket, gentlemen. That must be obvious to you. It's a deadly serious enterprise. So now we wait for a destroyer to escort us at sea. There are armed raiders in the Pacific; we must avoid them; we need to get where we're going, intact. If this operation succeeds, gentlemen, the outcome will be stunning beyond imagination.'

In the women's quarters, Kerry awoke. The ship was moving. She could hear her mother's voice full of sighs. 'Oh good, good, good, good.'

Jessie and Phoebe MacWhorter sat up simultaneously, as if moved by one brain and one impulse. 'Are we moving?' They asked the question of each other, and of their mother, and of everyone else.

'Yes. Yes. Yes. We're on the way.'

In the men's quarter's, Hogan felt sick. It had to be nerves. He couldn't be sea-sick yet.

Jon Griffiths wasn't sure whether he was panic-stricken or exhilarated.

Someone struck a match. A light switched on. About half-a-dozen men had already hit the deck. Others followed, reaching for overcoats, pulling on shoes or socks.

Jon tailed them into the corridor, up the iron steps, on to the open deck. There was a segment of moon. It was as cold as the devil. Hogan was there ahead of him. So was Kerry Shuffle. Jon couldn't see her, but sensed her

20

presence. Every time he thought of her, his nerves jumped.

They were moving down with the tide, a tug to either side, and nerves tingled to the scraping, the creaking, the throbbing engines.

'Where's the destroyer?'

'We're not likely to see it before the open sea.'

These were the fathers and mothers, the chosen ones of S.W.O.R.D. All around were their murmurs, their voices.

'Feels better already. It does, you know. Now we're moving. Now we're on the way.'

Yes, thought Hogan, with surface raiders waiting for us out in the Indian Ocean and the Pacific, sinking everything they take a fancy to.

That endless sea, thought Hogan. Those endless distances. The anguish of the chase. The anguish of high-explosive shells tearing everything to bits. The anguish of living with an imagination!

Submarines were out there, too, with torpedoes.

Your world blew up and getting to a lifeboat didn't mean you were lucky. You sat in the lifeboat and drifted. Perhaps you went nuts or died or drifted clear off the edge of the earth.

For year on top of year, each day of growing up had been like walking past the wall of an everlasting graveyard, an extra moon-shadow falling at your feet. Should have been one shadow – your own shadow – but there were two. The wall went on and on for miles and years and every time you glanced down the other shadow was still there.

In the schoolroom it was there. Teachers, not daring to understand fully for themselves, trying to explain.

In the field it was there, where you played a game; up or down a hundred thousand streets; in newspapers and weekly journals and on newsreel screens; always there. It never changed.

You'd see it in the faces of fellow-passengers on the train; you'd look across the table and it was there; you'd look in the mirror and it was there: the tension, the shadow.

Back when Austria broke, Adolf Hitler stood in his Mercedes Benz like Caesar in his chariot and drove into Vienna.

'*Heil mich. Heil mich.*'

Or something of the kind.

The tension was more than a feeling then, more than a word. It was the *knowledge* that something new was running loose, something different from the ordinary conflicts arranged by men.

In the mind the tension took the form of a pit, a visible thing, as if a rift were appearing in the Earth's surface, and Hitler at his whim could prop you at its brink and push.

Back when Czechoslovakia broke, the pit deepened, and if you were not wholly stupid you became aware of the greatness of the depths. Hogan needed no one to tell him.

Back when Poland broke, the future broke with it, the future into which you had hoped to grow day by day and year by year. There wasn't going to be a life for you. The future became the pit.

Then Denmark and Norway broke. And Holland and Belgium broke. And France broke, too.

Was there never to be an end to the collapse of nations?

The immovables you had been brought up to believe in, the foundations, the principles, the freedoms, the *armies*, were like imitations of wax left out in the heat.

In the pit were fires, were horrors, were matters beyond belief. If you fell in overnight, who'd get you out?

Any day now you'd wake to find Nazis in the streets. They were like creatures of the dark coming up out of holes while you slept.

The ship was moving from the river out into the channel, out into the Bay, and Kerry was in the war, a participant. And Hogan was in it. And Jon was in it. And Jessie and Phoebe were in it. And all the kids and all the grown-ups.

Kerry was on her ladder of sword-blades as never in her life before. It looked more like Jacob's ladder now.

22

Sword-blades one above the other reached sky high, reached all the way to Heaven.

At sea the destroyer was not waiting and the mothers of the babies held their infants closer.

'We may never actually sight the destroyer,' the Brigadier explained. 'Naval strategy works behind the scenes. But our defence is out there, mark my word.'

It wasn't, and he feared it wasn't.

Hogan found himself a hiding place that day, under a lifeboat, and started writing in an unused school exercise book. He called it 'Hogan Hancock's Doomsday Book'. Why should the Brigadier be the only one? And Kerry wrote in her tiny handwriting in her red diary. And Jon went on writing letters to his aunts and uncles and grandparents and mates at school, letters to go back to Australia with the ship, letters for the Navy censor to intercept and place in the cabinet marked S.W.O.R.D.

For fourteen days the ship plodded east and north at nine knots, as defenceless as a fat slug.

Three

(July 25, 1941)

Something changed, something to do with sound, motion, and personal security. Hogan knew about it almost before it happened; that was the nature of Hogan. Everyone else knew seconds later, except those a shipwreck would not have wakened.

'Jerusalem,' said Hogan's father, among half-a-dozen others, into the thick, all but suffocating darkness. 'What was that?'

The awful vulnerability of being human, below deck, in a rusty tub on the open sea!

The boiler's blown up, thought Hogan. Now we'll start drifting. Now I'll die, I bet.

Torpedo, thought Jon, wet with sweat.

In the women's quarters, the Oliver baby started caterwauling. She set off the Cunninghams' son, aged fifteen months. He set off his sister, aged five, and she set off Christopher McBride, the prodigy, who was seven, and wept daily because his piano was left behind. Jessie and Phoebe clutched for each other, as they usually did.

'We've stopped,' Hogan's father said, hopping on one leg, pulling on his trousers, thirty or forty others in that dreadful dormitory trying to do the same.

'It's 4.30 by my watch.'

'A quarter to five by me.'

All were waiting for the ship's siren, for the order to take to the lifeboats. It was a bleak, awful, hopeless feeling.

'Could we have dropped anchor?'

'I reckon we've hit a reef!'

Yeh, thought Hogan. The Pacific's full of reefs. We're on the Equator, I bet, high and dry. On a coral reef, I bet, and I can't swim fifty yards and it's three thousand miles home.

'We're there,' someone said. Sounded like Chambers, the old man, the Brigadier's batman from the 1914–18 war. 'The anchor always sounds like the end of the world in the middle of the night.'

We've survived, thought Jon. The anchor! I'm alive. That was the anchor going down, crashing through those holes. I never expected to get out of this lot in one piece.

The anchor, thought Hogan. Ain't that beautiful. I do love anchors.

Everyone was fumbling in the dark, fumbling through the blackout curtains, fumbling towards the companion-ways, fumbling up into starlight, barking shins, treading on toes, Jon hoping it might be Kerry getting crushed against him. It was someone else. But a lightening of spirit went with them.

'Quiet. Quiet. *Quiet*!' The Captain's voice carried almost fiercely from the bridge. 'Get those squawling children below. There's a war on, for God's sake.'

The 'squawling children' were taken back into the depths, the chatter became muted, voices dropped to something like a stage whisper.

Hogan was worrying about the need for quiet, because submarines had ears as big as African elephants, and being quiet now might be too late.

There was a sound that might have been breakers or wind in cornfields, but there wasn't a breath or a visible feature of land or sea. It was hot, sticky, and crystal black. There were stars of intense brilliance. The Southern Cross was low on the beam and on its back.

In the well-deck people swayed like a football crowd.

They began to see the cliff. Jon saw it clearly. His night vision was phenomenal. He saw Kerry, too, yards away. Kerry and the MacWhorter twins saw it. A cliff shaped like a wedge or a bladebone several hundred feet high. Hogan couldn't see a thing until his father traced the outline.

'There,' said Hogan's father, 'and won't I be cheerin' to get off this tub! I wonder where they've brought us?'

'Looks like Gibraltar,' said Mrs MacWhorter.

'Looks like a volcano.'

'Why would they bring us to a volcano?'

'Why not?'

'I don't like volcanoes.'

'You've never seen one.'

'Can anyone smell sulphur?'

'They're taking the lifeboat covers off.'

'Hell! What would they be doing that for?'

'I see breakers. Looks like a reef offshore.'

'Anything looking like a pier offshore?'

'There won't be any pier here. We'll run up the beach and lassoo a palm tree!'

Fascinating, thought Hogan, listening to grown adults working themselves into a fever.

'Ladies and gentlemen.' It was the Brigadier's voice, thank Heaven, coming from the bridge. 'Return without noise to your quarters and prepare to disembark. You're not expected to fall over each other in the dark, but check all port-hole covers and blackouts before allowing yourselves a minimum of light. We require the same security here as on the open sea. More so, for we become a stationary target. Make sure you leave nothing behind. Be ready to move at dawn. That's an hour. Hot drinks will be available from the galley from o-five hundred.'

It was uncomfortably like a dream. You were there, but you weren't. It was happening, but it wasn't. Though bruised by the closeness of everyone else, each person was alone and a little desperate.

Brothers and sisters and husbands and wives stood apart from each other. They had climbed the gangplank those long weeks ago and had started separating. In a week it had become a raging ache. You couldn't reach anyone any more, and unless you were Jessie or Phoebe you were afraid to try. The twins were specially privileged. Perhaps they were parts of the same soul.

This was to be the scene of Operation Sword, this barely-seen landfall. After six weeks on a stinking ship, this was it.

The whole incredible idea – this dream-like proposition – was lying off the stern waiting to happen. God alone knows how many went below muttering to themselves. Few were given to discussing their real feelings aloud any more.

Below deck, in places smelling like rabbit warrens, were disturbed babies and children, were distracted mothers and grandmothers and half-grown sisters trying to console them; were harassed fathers and grandfathers and half-grown brothers pushing from dormitory to dormitory and struggling up companion-ways with cabin baggage; were people looking vague leaning against anything that offered support, sipping sweet black tea from pannikins.

Above deck was the black equatorial night with its ten billion swaying stars; were the crewmen, surly as always, removing hatch covers and lowering boats; was the presence of the unnamed landfall with its dimly-seen cliff like a wedge or a bladebone.

This was the chosen place. For this the lives of a hundred persons had been turned upside-down.

Soon the sun would rise upon the chosen place and the chosen people would set foot upon it. Upon God alone knew what. Soon they would begin to mount guard or set watch; sky-watch, star-watch, day-long, night-long watch *for God alone knew what.*

Ideas that seemed reasonable when you were living at home in your own street looked different when you came face to face.

Four

(July 25, 1941)

At daylight there it was, shaping in the grey, forming in the glow, the great wedge-shaped mass of volcanic rock plunging from the dawn into the black Pacific depths, waves breaking where rock and sea met, a broad beach beginning there with long waves loping ashore. Beside the cliff and far beyond it lay dark forests of palms; no jetty, no smoke, no outrigger canoes, no Polynesians or Melanesians coming down to the water's edge.

'No houses,' said Hogan to his Dad.

'Jungle,' said his Dad, 'probably with boa constrictors.'

'Don't you know where we are, Dad?'

'Of course I don't know. How would I know? You're the brains of the family. Haven't you got pictures of it in your geography book?'

'No,' said Hogan.

'Stupid geography book. Cost me a fortune. Haven't you got a picture of it on one of your postage stamps?'

'No,' said Hogan.

'No one else knows either. Talk about an ignorant bunch of people.'

The sun came up, huge, red, and hot, and the first boatloads went over the side, down the rope ladders if they were able, lowered by manpower if they were not able.

'No one,' said the Brigadier, 'leaves the immediate beach area until I come ashore with Mr Chambers. Children must not be allowed out of sight. They may build castles or play ball, anything except get out of sight,

28

except leave the beach or enter the water. I repeat, no one is to wander out of sight until all personnel are accounted for, and all stores are ashore, and I am ashore also. It's the responsibility of the ship's crew to deliver the stores safely to land. After that, it's our responsibility to move them above the high-water mark. I anticipate the operation will take four hours.'

It took four hours.

'Getting onto this island,' said Hogan's Dad, 'is dead easy. You come roaring in like an express train. Getting back off it again might be a problem, unless they shoot us from a cannon.'

Kids, set free, were screaming up and down the beach, turning somersaults and cartwheels and leapfrogging, digging for crabs like dogs, making ten-league boots out of wet sand, with seaweed for laces and shells for holes, all yelling non-stop.

'Look at me, Mum. No hands! I'm standing on me head!'

'Is that a banana tree over there?'

'It's a coconut tree, you silly thing.'

'I say, that tree's got boils. I bet they hurt.'

'It's a breadfruit tree, nitwit, like in the adventure books.'

'Mum! Can I have some toast from the breadfruit tree for my breakfast?'

'You'll get a thick ear for your breakfast.'

'I heard you say my piano would be here.'

'If I eat that green thing will I get the bellyache?'

'If you eat that green thing you'll die. Hang on a minute, I'll cut you a slice.'

'I want to see the ladies that wear the grass skirts and go wobble-wobble.'

'You're not old enough to see that sort of thing.'

'I am!'

'I want my pack of cards. Who's for a game of gin rummy? I can't stand this fooling round out-of-doors.'

'You'll be fooling round out-of-doors, Buster, until doom cracks.'

'Can I go flounder-fishing, Dad?'

'The sharks'll do the fishing if you go out there.'

'Where are all the brown kids to teach us how to climb the palm trees? My missionary book's got brown kids in it without any pants on, lucky dogs.'

'Do you think the brown kids'll have a piano?'

'Crumbs,' said Hogan, 'aren't these little kids a trial? I just know I was never as bad. But it's nice being here, just the same, little kids and all. Could've been the South Pole. Well, it could have. Could have been icebergs and crevasses and flippin' penguins. They say penguins taste like urk. What's for breakfast?'

'Fingernails,' said his Dad.

Back and forth rowed the seamen, smoke drifting from the ship's funnel offshore, stores mounting on the beach.

Flour. Rice. Sugar. Salt. Tea. Coffee. Cocoa. Spices. Baking powder. Yeast. Canned beef. Canned fat. Dried milk. Soap. Seeds. Matches. The Union Jack. One barrel of nuts, bolts, screws, hinges and assorted ironmongery. A forge. Power kerosene. Lighting kerosene. Cooking utensils. Cutlery. Nails. Tools. Fencing wire. Rope. Twine. Leather. Paper. Books. Pencils. Bedding. Two wheelbarrows. The Australian flag. Paint. A pedal organ.

'I don't see my piano anywhere.'

'You can play the flamin' organ!'

Three fiddles. A guitar. Four nanny-goats. Guns. Ammunition. Fishing tackle. A bicycle. Lanterns. Candles. Suitcases. Cabin trunks. Tea-chests. Kit-bags. Pyrotechnics. Wire netting. Deck chairs. Mosquito netting. Four folding baby carriages. Two sewing machines. Two megaphones. Bolts of cloth. A trumpet. Surgical instruments. Medical supplies. One billy-goat. Radio transmitter/receiver. Battery charger. The Stars and Stripes. One hundred Rhode Island Reds. Four matching roosters. Tarpaulins. Bats. Balls. Empty glass jars and bottles.

'Come for a walk?' Jon said to Kerry.

She was helping her mother with the inventory and shook her head. There wasn't a boy on the planet who'd walked the length of a block with Kerry Shuffle.

'We'll come,' said Jessie and Phoebe, 'though we mustn't get out of sight, worse luck.'

They ranged up and down the beach, peering into the sun-splashed shadows. Didn't look as though a living soul had set foot among the palms for a couple of centuries. Didn't look like the place for lovely brown maidens in grass skirts or golden South Sea island youths either. Looked exactly like the place for Bengal tigers.

The Brigadier rowed ashore with Mr Chambers in a ten-foot dinghy which they pulled up after them out of the water.

'We say all stores are present and correct. Do you confirm this, Mrs Shuffle?'

'No umbrellas, Brigadier.'

'What umbrellas might they be?'

'For the monsoon, Brigadier.'

'Anyone fool enough to venture into the monsoon, madam, will have to make his own arrangements. Do we have our people, Mr Hawkins?'

'All present and correct, Brigadier.'

'Fire the *all-clear*, Bert.'

Mr Chambers raised the Verey pistol and shrieks from the children greeted the brilliant green stars with their arcs of smoke exploding seawards. They seemed to hang there until an Aldis lamp answered from the ship's bridge, though the ship appeared to be moving in the same instant. Hogan could have sworn it. Anchor stowed in readiness, no doubt, black smoke blooming above.

'That's that,' said Hogan's Dad, along with about twenty others, though he alone said it loud enough to be generally heard. 'Off and away like a startled hare.'

A hundred souls, there they were, with the foreseeable needs for survival, marooned on a foreign shore. What shore?

'Hallelujah,' called the Everard family, old man Everard leading by a second, as he used to do in the Bijou Theatre in the old days back home.

Hallelujah about what? thought Hogan.

Jon's father began to clap. So all the Griffiths's clapped, Jon feeling sheepish for a few moments only, because everyone else started clapping, too, the small children jumping with excitement. Everything was so special, so mysteriously grown-up. All the grown-ups were clapping. All the sprats imitated them.

Hogan clapped, grimacing, wondering what he felt, sighing about himself, meaning it despite himself.

Kerry clapped, smiling at her beautiful Brigadier.

Jessie and Phoebe clapped, glowing, laughing at each other, as if to say, 'It's marvellous to be alive together, to be in it together, *to be here together*.'

It was marvellous standing on their unknown shore, high and dry, committed to the great mission, a hundred souls clapping as the steamer moved away. The impossible had happened. The impossible took longer. The impossible was *here*.

'God Save the King,' shouted the Brigadier.

They sang the National Anthem with voices among them that had graced chorales and choirs, and with boys who shrieked on one note and croaked on the next.

It was marvellous, marvellous.

It was like being in the Bijou again on that incredible afternoon. The emotions of that afternoon came flooding back with the same fervour.

They sang the second verse of the National Anthem and sang it mightily.

This is living a great experience, thought Kerry. When it's great, you know it. I'll remember it till I die.

Five

(July 25, 1941)

The Brigadier stood in their midst upon the shore, head and shoulders above them. 'Welcome to Tangu Tangu. We're almost astride the Equator. Admiralty Islands lie south and the New Guinea mainland lies beyond that, and they're both about as far as you'd ever want to row.

'The War Cabinet ordered that our destination should be kept a secret. I'm sorry it's troubled you, as I know it has, but without the Prime Minister's approval, we'd never have got here. Never. Never. Never in a hundred years. Of the ship's complement, only the officers know where we have been put down, and the crew was chosen for its ignorance of these waters. We might be forgiven for imagining that the crew was chosen for its ignorance in general. I must agree they were a rare bunch.

'We were aboard our ship for forty days and forty nights. The classic wilderness period of scripture. An exceptional period, you must agree, bringing remarkable images to mind. It was not designed to happen that way. I expected to leave port within the week and hoped for a ship with a few more knots and for a crew with a few more social graces. But they got us here, God bless 'em, so let's forget the irritations and insults. Let each of us feel the joyful enthusiasm, the sense of privilege, the wonder of our great beginning in the Bijou when Operation Sword began.'

Standing there listening to him was marvellous. And there went the ship, trailing its black cloud, farther out to sea, farther south, out of their lives.

I don't know, thought Hogan. Is me Dad not the idiot he thinks he is for getting us into this?

The Brigadier was still talking, if 'talking' was a fair word. 'Utterance' would be nearer the mark.

'My friends, the unoccupied Tangu Tangu mission station lies close to the opposite shore at about half-a-mile. We walk into it by permission of the Australian Government which administers the territory.

'Over there on the north side we'll find a hut of some kind for every family, with huts to spare for special activities, and a meeting hall and cleared space adequate for our needs – or so I believe. With little difficulty we'll be self-supporting in a short time. All sorts of exotic fruits grow profusely, as you can see. And our vegetable garden we plant tomorrow, *if* we don't manage to plant it today.

'You gardeners are in for a real experience. Drop the seeds in the ground and leap clear. The Reverend Pearce, whom you met at the Bijou, tells me that fertility here in his time was staggering. Crop after crop after crop. Let's hope the magic hasn't departed with the people. It's true the mission station is unoccupied, or we wouldn't be here. A better word might be *abandoned*. Well, we'll see what that means. To the best of my knowledge not a soul but ourselves presently inhabits this island over some forty-four square miles. You may be curious about it.

'These Pacific populations shift, they tell me. Every now and then they build a few more canoes and sail off into the sunset. Give it a moment's thought and you'll see we've done much the same ourselves, and who knows, but for a similar reason.

'A beautiful island they've left us, my friends. Something like every man and woman's dream of Paradise. And in the native language they call that wonderful cliff up there 'Seat of the Watcher for God'. How's that for a nice bit of symbolism?

'Let me say something to you children and young people.You're not here *in tow* with your parents. In some cases your parents have been chosen because of you.

'I know what being a child means. I know a surprising

34

amount about it. I was the same kind of kid as you. I'm one of the fortunate few who remembers. But I tell you, no matter how much from time to time you wonder about yourself, you can speak to God more directly than the grown-ups. When you're grown up you'll come to know what I mean. Try hard to give us grown-ups your love, even though we drive you crazy from time to time. We have turned sometimes apathetic and sometimes cynical. These are the sins of the world, the frightened sins, the great sins that are not to be found in you.

'I doubt if there's a prayer under Heaven stronger than a child's prayer, or more able to claim God's attention. Many desperate calls from grown-ups in the very near past have got nowhere. Almost the whole world has prayed for deliverance from the great evil that has spawned in Europe. You're here to give special energy to the calls that we make. Beautiful children brought to a beautiful island to call upon God to save the world from this evil that's destroying the civilising labour of hundreds of generations of men and women.

'My dear kids, it's *stunning* that S.W.O.R.D. by beating at the Government's door has forced the Government to allow this to happen; that S.W.O.R.D. comes here as God's servant to invoke His aid. We believe God promised thousands of years ago that He would come at the end of the world to save His people – if His people put their lives in order and called to Him. We are here, on behalf of the nation, to test the promise.'

Six

(July 25, 1941)

By candlelight that evening, Hogan wrote in his Doomsday Book – for as long as he could endure the mosquitoes,
for as long as he could hold his head up, for as long as his
mother was prepared to tolerate the annoyance of the
flickering flame and the smell of scorching moths. All
provisions coincided.

'Go to bed, Hogan. *At once.*'

Bed was one blanket and the earth floor of the hut. His
pillow was a folded towel. He burned with bites from head
to foot. The mosquitoes bit through his shirt, bit through
his trousers, bit through his shoes and socks. If they
propagated malaria, he was as dead as a duck!

There were centipedes. There were spiders. There were
unspeakable insects that crawled and crept and wriggled
and writhed and flew in circles round his head.

Tangu Tangu was an entomologist's reward for a
virtuous life.

'How did they all get here, for gawd's sake?'

'How did what get here?' his mother asked.

'The bloody insects. There are billions of 'em.'

'Shhh,' she said. 'You'll wake your father.'

Hogan had written in his Doomsday Book an entry that
went something like this:

> The trek through the jungle to the mission station took most
> of the day, although it wasn't a mile. Heaven knows why we
> landed on the southern shore instead of the northern one.

Stupid. Tides, maybe? I don't know. Ours is not to reason why. Ours is to bally well suffer.

We had to cut a path with axes, hatchets and machetes to get the stores through. Murder it was. Mr Tregellas got hurt. I think he thought he was Errol Flynn having a sword fight. Dr Weatheral had to give him eighteen stitches and Mrs MacWhorter held his hand. I think Mrs MacWhorter and Mr Tregellas have got something going. It's an ill wind, they say, that doesn't blow someone a bit of good, though I can't imagine why Mr Tregellas would want to have anything going with Mrs MacWhorter. Or with Jessie or Phoebe MacWhorter either, come to think of it. Imagine giving them a kiss. Urk. They'll never get married unless Mrs MacWhorter gives them away with free motor-cars.

Cutting through that jungle was a bit of a shock for the Brigadier, I think. He lost a lot of his bounce. He might be right about the vegetables though. Everything grows like crazy. You'd think it was one of those Inca places in South America, all swamped in jungle. I never knew there were so many coconut trees. Busting out of every rooftop and every heap of dirt. Found two coconut trees four feet tall growing right here inside this hut. Had to pull them up before we could sit down.

The Brigadier was real taken aback by the derelict look. I think everyone's worrying about why the people who lived here went away, because there's a beach as good as you'd ever want to see and enough free fruit to fill every hut to the rafters. Flowers growing everywhere. Little pigs scampering about in the bushes. Though the way the Brigadier feels about pork being unhealthy, I expect these little pigs will be left to scamper to their heart's content. Wild fowl, too. Black Orpingtons, would you believe, living in the trees. Fancy bringing Rhode Island Reds with us. We'll have Rhode Island Blacks and Red Orpingtons running everywhere.

Why did everyone go away? Is the water poisoned or something? Is there some filthy disease? Well, there aren't any bodies lying around; no skeletons under the floorboards or anything. There aren't any floorboards, unless the termites have eaten them.

Seven

(July 26, 1941)

Jon's interview with the Brigadier on shipboard did not cost him the 'special job' on Tangu Tangu. He got it, *with knobs on*, as the Brigadier might have said. Exactly half of it. Hogan got the other half.

'I promise to remain awake,' Jon said, on the day the promises were made, July 26, 1941.

There he was, stretching out a hand to the open Bible and everyone was standing around, one hundred souls. He was promising to remain awake at night, maybe forever! The idea was *appalling*.

Everyone was looking at him, his parents, his kid brother, Jessie and Phoebe, Kerry.

There he was, promising to stay awake until the world ended.

Hogan was beside him with a hand to the other page, and by chance the Bible fell open at the Book of Daniel, chapters eleven and twelve. Well, if anything in this world happens by chance.

Jon saw the Brigadier frown.

Perhaps the Bible opened there because the Brigadier read from it often, but he read often from other places, too.

'We swear no oaths,' he then said. 'The Bible tells us that God doesn't require fancy words, just a promise. But having given the promise, each of us lives with the responsibility of keeping it. The strictest discipline is that imposed by the honest person upon himself, for it is not a trained response or a mindless twitch. Being on one's own honour is the absolute honour.'

That was the substance of his utterance in front of the main gathering – for everyone, even the young children, had made promises. Promises to be as good as possible. Promises never to wander. Promises never to enter the sea unattended. And there were promises of uncomplaining *gladsome* service from everyone old enough to prepare food or weave split bamboo or drive a nail.

'Failing one's own self,' the Brigadier said, 'is the absolute failure.' But he added refinements for Hogan and Jon after they set out for the Seat of the Watcher for God.

First he said, 'Mr Chambers, you'll accompany us with a wheelbarrow. Kindly bring a tarpaulin, two blankets, and a tomahawk. Lads, you have fifteen minutes to get your things together. Bare essentials only. Say goodbye to your families.'

Fifteen minutes! It was like trying to catch a train that had gone.

'It's impossible,' wailed Jon, tearing through the chaos of the family hut. Nothing was properly unpacked. Everything was locked in trunks or lying in heaps. No one knew where anything was. 'There are things I've got to have.'

'You're only going for tonight.'

'Like hell and the rest of it.'

'You're not to swear,' his mother said.

'I'm not swearin'. I'm desperate. Where's me sunhat? You know how easy I get sunstroke. I'll never pass my exams. I haven't looked at a text book for two months. And I want my copy of *Jurgen*.'

'You're going less than a mile, Jon. You're not going to Peru. You'll be back tomorrow.'

'I won't be back tomorrow. You heard the Brigadier. Did he say I'd be back? Where's my copy of *Jurgen*?'

'You'd be better employed looking for changes of underwear. For Heaven's sake go sit in a corner and leave it to me.'

'Did you hear him say I've got to stay awake? For how long do I stay awake? Till one o'clock? Till two o'clock? How long does he mean?'

'He'll tell you, Jon, in his own good time.'

'Every night, he said. It's not natural. How am I going to stay awake every night?'

'You'll manage.'

'I've never stayed awake for a single night in my whole life. Three o'clock in the morning. Once.'

'Gladsome service for God, Jon. You promised.'

'It's all right for you people singing hymns and mending holes in socks. You can be gladsome doing that. How can you be gladsome staying awake every night? It'll stunt me growth. I'll get bags under me eyes.'

'You're a picture of health and six feet tall.'

'I'm five feet eleven and three-quarters and I'll go cross-eyed. You watch. I'll end up like Hogan. Did you find my copy of *Jurgen*?'

'I'll send it on.'

'Is that a promise? You're always putting it away somewhere. You don't like me reading it; I know you. You'll send me the Bible instead.'

'I'll send it on with your razor and toothbrush.'

'What do I want a toothbrush for? I'll never eat again. Did he say anythin' about eating? No. What do I want a razor for? Who's going to care what I look like? Anyway, I've had me shave for this week. Did you hear him say I've got to stay awake at night? No wonder he wanted to build me up with all those exercises. Serve him right, old Heracles never answered my letter. *Every night, he said*. I'll go mental.'

The Brigadier took Jon and Hogan to the top of the great cliff, to the place called 'Seat of the Watcher for God'. Mr Chambers stayed behind on the lower slopes to unload the wheelbarrow and to erect a temporary shelter. He was an expert at pitching tents; he'd been at it for seventy years.

Behind them, below them, lay the isthmus and the mission station at fifteen hundred yards or more, back where the island fanned out like the head of a tennis racket. So oddly-shaped and oddly-contoured. Coming from the distance were the sounds of hammers and saws

40

and the shrieks of children. They could see about forty square miles of jungle with isolated areas of grassland. There were rocky crags and wheeling flocks of birds. There was a vast ocean and a vast sky. There were unbelievable hues of silver, gold and blue.

The Brigadier said, 'From here you can see to eternity. Day or night the same. Others may pray or prophesy or attend to our physical wellbeing. Your duty is here. In your charge I place the ultimate responsibility of signalling the coming of the Heroes of Light, or whatever else God sends. Even if skies are overcast, even if cloud caps the cliff, even if the moment on hand seems the most unlikely since the world began, seeing to eternity is why you're here.

'We'll put a sentry hut at the foot of the slope, with a personal bunk, a personal desk, and a personal chair for each of you, though you'll never be there together. Together up here, perhaps, but never down there.

'Up here we'll place a booth to keep off the sun and the rain and site the old village drum for signalling. You're on duty always as from now, both of you, as the captain of a ship or an aeroplane is always on duty, as the King's guard is always on duty. It's a holy vow. You've promised to watch and to wait, just as priests promise chastity and obedience.

'I see you as priests; I see myself as the abbot. Which means you obey me. Which means that you up here allow the girls down there to live their own lives without your generous assistance. Do I make myself clear?'

Never clearer, gloomed Jon.

'All your energies and concentration,' said the Brigadier, 'are to be directed into maintaining a wakeful watch. You, Jon, have the night watch. Hogan, the day. They are not interchangeable. I'll personally inspect each watch, day and night, from now until the end. Those for whom we wait will come without warning. I'll come without warning also. Every now and then I'll come twice. Do I make myself clear?'

'Absolutely, sir,' said Jon.

'Yes, sir,' said Hogan.

'Generally, you'll see no one but me, or Mr Chambers who'll be servicing your larder and laundry. Everyone else will be forbidden to communicate with you except in my presence. You'll come down to camp once a week for worship and for a Sabbath celebration meal with your families at my table. Mr Chambers will occupy the look-out position during your absence. But accidents happen. Little children wander. People become ill. I may be required for one reason or another to relieve you temporarily from duty. Inevitably, sooner or later, you'll find yourself alone with someone. When that occurs, you may discuss your pimples or the weather. Nothing else. Is that clear?'

'Sir!' said Jon.

'Yes, sir,' said Hogan.

'There's one other matter of which you'll say nothing until you learn that it's common knowledge. I speak of why Tangu Tangu is deserted and of why the cliff has its odd name. The earth and its forces used to be the gods round here. Real red-blooded stuff. The Reverend Pearce is of the opinion that the old beliefs died hard and that Christianity got put on or taken off like a hat. That once the people walked out of the church doors they went dashing joyfully back to the jungle.

'Tangu Tangu is volcanic. And alive. With knobs on, lads. With brass knobs on. A lot of islands are like it in these parts, like bubbles on boiling oil. When the gods threaten retribution, the locals don't argue, because retribution is what they're always expecting. For very good reason, I imagine. Then they wrap up their loin cloths in a banana leaf and head for the horizon. This is known as expediency! There was a real nice earthquake here four years ago. Lasted, on and off, for about three weeks, and the Reverend Pearce suddenly found himself sitting alone twiddling his thumbs. So he took home leave. And we're here because beggars can't be choosers!'

For a second or two the Brigadier looked almost coy.

'I say to you lads, watch for the local god as well as the

Great God. Strikes me they have a strong understanding. At the first sign of one or the other, start beating that drum. Hit it like your pulse-beat, as fast as you can hit it! We'll have some decisions to make and quick ones. If you sight aircraft or submarines or ships, beat it at intervals of about three seconds. They may be friendly. But they may not be. The responsibility of decision doesn't lie with you, but the responsibility of sighting and seeing and warning the rest of us does lie with you.'

Hogan was alone on the cliff.

Suddenly, Hogan was on watch.

The Brigadier walked away with Jon down the rocky slope. Four hundred yards of it, like the face of a wedge, before denser vegetation began. There the tent erected by Mr Chambers was taking shape. Was the slope ashen? Hogan hadn't stood on a volcano rim before. If this were part of the rim, it must have been a small part. Where was the rest of it? Those crags in the distance, with everything in between blown to Kingdom Come? When had that occurred? A hundred years ago? Three or four hundred years ago? How quickly had this feverish jungle healed the wounds?

'Gawd,' Hogan said aloud. 'Twelve hours a day up here on me lonesome. That's every day he's talking about. That's *all* day he's talking about. I'll go nuts. I'll turn into a grease spot. I'll fry like an egg.'

Eight

(July 26 — 27, 1941)

Jon couldn't see his wrist watch. Well, the shape of it was there, more or less, but the luminous face didn't 'luminate'. It was a remarkable invention. The harder you peered at it, the more invisible it became. Like the dodo, galloping in ever-diminishing circles. For thirty-five weeks back home, at sixpence a week, he'd whitewashed the lines of the local tennis court to earn the price of it.

Talk about waste your substance on riotous whitewashing. Talk about exploitation of the innocent.

The only way you could make the stupid watch work was hold it up to the sun then rush into a dark room. Which in broad daylight was a demented activity and was an impossibility at night. On the dial it said, 'Made in Switzerland', but you just *knew* the Japanese had changed the name of a little town outside Tokyo and called it *Switzerland*, same as they called other towns *Sheffield* and *U.S.A.*

Was it two o'clock? Or three o'clock?

He ate his first supper. Every crumb. And ate his second supper. Every crumb. And consumed his bananas. And emptied his thermos flask and his army-type water bottle.

Was it for ever and ever? And then amen?

Glory. The agony of staying awake. Like a torture straight out of the Thousand and One Nights. Pinching yourself. Talking to yourself. Punching yourself. Jumping up and down. Running back and forth. 'And take it easy,

44

sonny Jim, you can't run too far or you'll run clear off the edge of this here cliff, head over turkey, down and down and down.'

A paralysing thought, Jon David Griffiths. God's gift to the female sex, if only they had the wit to realize it, smeared all over the seaboard like a blot of ink. And who'd know? Who'd care? There they all were, tucked up in their cosy little cots a mile away, snoring their heads off. There was Hogan even, under his bit of tarpaulin, saying his prayers, 'Oh thank you, thank you, thank you so very much that I'm not up there on the cliff in the middle of the night running round in circles like Jon Griffiths trying to stay awake.'

So he'd concentrate on a star, a nice little red star that wasn't over bright. 'You can keep your white ones. You can keep your yellow ones. Who wants a gimlet in his head?' Soft red star. Pretty red star. Soon he'd go cross-eyed like Hogan and his nice red star would totter round until there were fifty little red stars, oddly-shaped little stars looking like dashes or commas or exclamation marks. He'd bang himself on the head, a hand to either side, his brains in the middle, and there'd be one star again, a nice little red star, and a sore head everywhere else.

There was a good thing about it though. He wasn't being shot at. And it had to be better than getting a bayonet in your belly or a grenade down the back of your neck or a thundering great tank driving over the top of you like you were a lump of road metal. Being a sentry waiting for God had that licked. Yeh, man.

Whereupon his eyelids would close with total deter-mination, as if he had a fifty-pound dead weight attached to each. His conscience might tolerate this infamy for perhaps ten seconds, then his neck would crack and the roots of his hair would shriek in protest. Each individual hair. Each root. And his stomach would detach itself from the rest of his insides and rotate like an ice-cream churn.

'Is it four o'clock? Or five o'clock? How long's the sun going to be before it sticks its nose up? Is it ever going to

45

come up again? I reckon someone's taken the plug out. The blanky thing's sunk. Me eyes are stickin' out on stalks. They're dangling on me chest. How did I get meself into this? Awake. Awake. Wide awake. Oh grief, I'm going to throw up, I think. I'm going to bring up the inner soles of me feet.

'Why can't he mount the guard like the army does it? Why can't he change watch every two hours? *Twelve hours* is like the Inquisition. It's like having your fingernails pulled out. And it's tomorrow night, too. And the night after that. And the week after that. Yes, yes, I'm marching up and down. I'm awake. I'm being a good boy. Left-right. Left-right. I'll be stuck up here when I'm on the old-age pension. I'll have a beard three feet long with birds' nests in it. I'll do me exercises. I'll touch me toes. One-two. One-two. One-two.'

'That's the spirit,' said the Brigadier.

There he was! Materialized! Cane tucked under his arm! All six-feet-ten of him! Come to inspect the guard! Half a pace from Jon's nose and Jon hadn't heard a thing.

'Sir!'

'Wide awake, Jon?'

'Absolutely. Sir!'

'Anything to report, Jon?'

'Not a thing. Sir!'

'Coping with the situation, Jon?'

'Loving it. Sir!'

'Well done. You're half-way there. It's the attitude of mind that passes the time so quickly. O-one-thirty already. Goodnight to you, Jon.'

'Goodnight. Sir!'

It was totally night again. Totally silent again. Except for the sea. God knows what that man wore on his feet. You couldn't even hear him walk away. You couldn't even be sure he'd gone. Had he been there all the time? An appalling thought. Bet your life he'd been there all the time. Bet your life he was still there. And it was only half-past-one. Not four o'clock. Not five o'clock. Not

46

going on for six. Half-past-one!

Jon wanted to cry.

'SIR!'

Jon bellowed into the night! He couldn't think of anything else to do.

A blue light.

'SIR. QUICK. A LIGHT.'

A blue light offshore. Miles away. Faint. Winking.

'Grief. What do I do? I haven't got me drum to bang.'

The Brigadier's command came sharply up the slope. 'Be quiet! Put your binoculars on it!'

Binoculars.

Where were the binoculars? He couldn't find them.

They were hanging round his neck.

He couldn't *see* through the binoculars. It was like putting his head in a bag. Like peering through a blocked-up keyhole. Couldn't find the light anywhere. He bruised several eyelashes into one eye and had to close the eye tightly. Couldn't see the light then, even without the binoculars.

'Give them to me!'

He tore them off, grateful to be rid of the hateful things, and thrust them at the Brigadier, grinding the heel of his palm into his right eye, vainly trying to see out of his left eye, wondering how it could be that everything in the world always went wrong for Jon David Griffiths.

'Where *is* the blasted light?'

'Other end of the island. North side, sir.'

'These glasses are useless. What've you been doing with the focus? No human being could ever see out of them. . . A ship. Well, there it is.'

'Ours?' said Jon timidly, after a sheepish pause. 'Sir?'

'How could it be ours? Use your brains. All of thirty-six hours since it left us. It's a freighter of about 4000 tons. Coming very close in. Must be sure of themselves, by God. Must know the waters. . .'

Jon squinted into the dark distance, rubbing at two smarting eyes, and couldn't see a thing.

'No lights,' said the Brigadier. 'No blue light either. No

47

identification that I can pick up. Fascinatin'. Hard to pick anything up.'

'Is it a German raider, sir?'

'Could be, by Jove. Coming in for fresh water. No one's lived here for years and the blighters would know it. Thank God they're up the other end, Jon. Down this end they'd have given us a problem. All we've got is a couple of pea-shooters. What do you see with the naked eye?'

'I've got eyelashes, sir. Eyelashes in me eye.'

'God,' said the Brigadier, 'put seventeen-year-old eyes on watch and they get eyelashes in them. *Get the eyelashes out of them!* And get Hogan out of bed and send him up to me. And get on down to that camp faster than you can run. Every able-bodied man out, with a weapon in hand, axe, club, rifle, stick, or a piece of rock. Hawkins in command. He'll straighten them up. Every man standing by at the meeting hall, quietly, calmly. God knows how we'll manage that, but no lights, no noise, no panic, no women, no kids. Make that clear to Hawkins. Understood?'

'Yes, sir.'

'Off you go.'

Twenty strides downhill the Brigadier's voice stopped him.

'Come back!'

Back he scuttled, and the Brigadier said, 'I'd swear a dinghy's rowed out from shore. They're picking up a party. Fascinatin'. Pickin' up a party at that end because we've come in at this end! Hold off from Hawkins, boy. Good work, catching that little light. They're not German. Germans would have chopped us up. These characters don't want to be seen. Don't want to be compromised! Take a look for yourself.'

'No, no, sir. Please. I don't want the binoculars. I see much better without them.'

'Rubbish. If you see better without them, tell me what's happening.'

'I don't know, sir. I can't see that far.'

'You'll *learn* how to use these things, boy. You'll

48

practise constantly until the use of them is instinctive.'

'Yes, sir.'

'Your light originated from the dinghy, I think. Probably wasn't showing above a second or two. So you may *see* adequately with the naked eye, but you *search* with binoculars. In conditions of minimal light I'm able to view the scene in detail. Do I make the point?'

'Yes, sir.'

'Well, what do you think it's about?'

'I think someone got a fright sir, when we arrived.'

'Yes.'

'And signalled to be taken off.'

'Almost certainly.'

'It's a depot ship, even though it's not German, you say.'

'That's what I say, Jon.'

'So they've got to be Japanese, sir. Like a survey party.'

'We're not at war with the Japanese.'

'But they're friends of Hitler, sir.'

'So Operation Sword is not the secret we've supposed it to be? Is that what you're suggesting?'

'They might never have heard of S.W.O.R.D., sir, but I bet they know now that a hundred people are here.'

'Good lad. So I'll brief Hogan about it. Then I'll decide who else is to be told, and how much. I'm asking you to keep your hat on it. . . There they go. Chugging out to sea. Japanese, almost certainly. I hope that's the last we see of them.'

Nine

Operation Sword, Tangu Tangu,
Routine Orders,
Monday to Saturday:

06.30	Reveille. Curfew lifted.
06.36	Roll call. Daily Routine Orders. (Mr Hawkins.)
06.45	Ablutions.
07.00	Breakfast.
07.30	Morning Prayer Parade. (Brigadier.)
08.00–12.00	Work Parade. Duties as posted in Daily Routine Orders.
09.00–12.00	School Parade. (Mrs Shuffle.)
10.00–12.00	Sick Parade. (Dr Weatheral. Sister Weatheral.)
11.00–12.00	Brigadier's hour. Interviews by appointment.
12.15	Midday Prayer Parade. (Brigadier.)
12.30	Lunch.
13.00	News and Information. (Mr Hawkins.)
13.30	Physical Culture Parade. (Mr Cunningham.)
14.00	Work Parade. Children's Rest Period.
16.00	Family Free Time.
18.00	Dinner.
19.00	Evening Prayer Parade. (Brigadier.)
20.00	Family Free Time.
22.00	Lights Out.
24.00	Curfew.

SUNDAY: The Sabbath shall be observed.
The Sabbath Day Celebration Dinner shall
begin at 17.00 hours.

Matthew Palmer,
Brigadier,
27 July, 1941.

Ten

(July 27, 1941 — August 21, 1941)

Night after night after night, there Jon was, fighting himself awake, Griffiths versus Griffiths, twelve one-hour rounds. And no new sightings of lights to wake him up again. So he had Mr Chambers bring extra suppers to the sentry hut. And more bananas. And two vacuum flasks of coffee. Just as well the MacWhorter twins found some coffee trees to boost the ration. Well, they were something like coffee trees. Better than discovering gold.

Each afternoon at 5.45 he packed his little bag and set off to climb the cliff accompanied by seagulls. At the top would be his exciting twice-daily encounter.

'Hi, Hogan.'

'Hi, Jon.'

'How's your grandmother?'

'How's your wooden leg?'

'See anything interesting?'

'Saw you coming.'

Having disposed of Hogan, he'd estimate wind speed and direction by observing the wind lanes or the whitecaps on the sea, check the state of the tide, and settle down yogi fashion to supervise the sunset. By taking a very firm stand with the sun over a period of several weeks he was able to move its point of departure several degrees closer to the Equator. He gave thought, too, to the moon's orbit and to the relative positions of the constellations and was able to effect several useful improvements.

Each night, sometimes once, sometimes twice, the Brigadier *materialized*.

Even when the moon was bright and you could see the crests of the waves offshore, even when you could pick out palm trees at a quarter of a mile, that man *materialized*. Fifty years if he was a day; as agile as a fly on the ceiling. Two hundred and forty pounds if he was an ounce; as light-footed as a moth. He must have had a magic lamp.

'Good evening, Jon.'

'Good evening. Sir!'

And your heart would hit your ribs like a fettler's hammer belting pegs into railway lines. Your breath would catch from the shock of it.

'Nothing to report?'

'Nothing to report. Sir!'

'How many suppers tonight, Jon?'

'Three. Sir!'

'Caesar! Already?'

'One and a half so far. Sir! One and a half still to go.'

'How many bananas, Jon?'

'Stuffed to the ears with them. Sir!'

'Jolly good. How much do you weigh this week, Jon?'

'A hundred and thirty-eight pounds. Sir!'

'Excellent. Excellent. I told you bananas would do it. Look what they did to me. Used to stand four feet tall. Used to weigh fifty pounds.'

'I find that difficult to believe, Sir!'

'True, Jon. True as I stand here. I was six years old at the time. Good evening to you, lad.'

'Good evening. Sir!'

And away he'd go. And suddenly wouldn't be there. Or would appear not to be there. But who could be sure? Hogan said he came on his bike and leant it against the sentry hut wall. And later would go away.

'How much later?'

'I dunno. Night-time's my sleeping time. Do you keep check on him in the daytime for me?'

'Daytime's *my* sleeping time. I can't see in the daylight. I'm turning into an owl. I'm nocturnal. Me hair's going pink.'

Keeping awake. Keeping awake. . .

I'm doing handstands,
Perfect handstands,
Even though I fall off the top
In a heap.
If I could see
Where I was going
I'd do cartwheels
And that'd set you back in your seat.
Say,
Who wants a gorgeous kiss?
Come on,
You beautiful maidens,
Roll up, roll up.
Sixpence for a slobber on your right cheek,
And sixpence for a slobber on your left,
But if you want it in the middle
On your kisser
It'll cost you your reputation
At least.
I'm Griffiths,
Griffiths South Pacific,
Griffiths the Terrific,
Griffiths the Magnific,
Griffiths the Horrific,
The terror of every girl in the street.
I wear me hat sideways
And me beard grows a foot in a week.
I'm the roughest and the toughest,
I'm the very, very worst,
I'm a thoroughly disreputable lump,
And every maid that I see
Goes weak at the thought
That she might get a kiss
From me.
I wine 'em and I dine 'em
And I toast 'em and I roast 'em
And they line up in their queues
For me wink.

I'm very, very horrible,
I'm terrible, I'm terrible,
I'm the Curse of King Edward Street.

'Hullo.'

Jon's heart almost stopped. He threw his hands to his ears in unbelief.

'You stupid girls,' he shrieked. 'What are you doing here?'

'Oh, charming,' said a voice out of the night. 'What a charming boy he is.'

'Go away, you two. You horrible twins. I'll be shot.'

'No one knows we're here,' said the voice out of the night, 'and we're not going to shoot you. Are you going to shoot yourself?'

'I'll bet you the Brigadier knows, I'll bet you, I'll bet you. He knows everythin', sooner than it happens.'

'The Brigadier,' said Jessie or Phoebe, as they sat themselves in front of him, 'has gone peddling on his bike back to his hut. Now he'll be reading his Bible or something. Or writing in his Doomsday Book. He rode straight past us. We could have reached out and given him a heart attack. He's going to fall off that bike one of these nights. He's going to hurt himself real bad. Our Mum doesn't know either. She's gone for a walk.'

'At this hour of the night?'

'It's only eleven o'clock. Lots of people go for walks at eleven o'clock. She's gone for a walk with Mr Tregellas.'

'Lucky him,' said Jon. 'And what about his nephew then?'

'Young Alan wouldn't know whether it's breakfast or teatime. He's sound asleep in bed like all the other little kids.'

'You've got to go this very moment, I'm tellin' you. Because the Brigadier'll come back.'

'We brought you a nice piece of toffee. It's the last we're allowed to make. It uses too much sugar.'

'You've got to go,' Jon wailed. 'Right now. Immediate. I promised no girls. I promised no hanky-panky. I bet you

55

had to promise, too.'

'Don't you want your toffee? It's the best we've ever made. It's hardly sticky at all until you start chewing.'

'*Oh do go.*'

'That's not the way to treat your friends,' Jessie or Phoebe said. 'We're the only friends you've got. Out of sight, out of mind, you know. No good being stuck on Kerry. She's only got eyes for him.'

'Him who? Who's him?'

'The Brigadier.'

'Come off it,' said Jon. 'What would he want with a little girl?'

'She's not little. Girls her age get married. Girls our age get married. Pity you weren't twins.'

'Thank Heaven I'm not,' said Jon.

'You're very rude to us.'

'If you don't go away I'll call for help.'

'Who are you going to call? Hogan? He'd run for his life. He's scared of girls.'

'So am I.'

'No one knows we're here. You're quite safe.'

'I'm the very opposite of safe.'

'We're not holding hands or anything, are we? We're not kissing you or anything. And you must be able to see the Brigadier coming from half-a-mile off.'

'You *can't* see him coming. He comes up out of fissures in the ground. And you can't hear him coming either. All you can hear is the sea. Oh please go away. I'm on guard. I'm on watch. I've got a very important job. Or did he send you up himself to tempt me?'

'He didn't.'

'I've only got your word for it.'

'The Brigadier wouldn't do a thing like that. He's a gentleman.'

'He can't be much of a gentleman if he's chasing Kerry.'

'He's not chasing Kerry. She's chasing him. Great big oggle eyes. She's the one that's not being the gentleman.'

'And you're not being ladies. You'll be getting me into

56

trouble. When have I done anything to hurt you?'

'Never, worse luck,' said Jessie and Phoebe. Then went away.

Goodness, thought Jon.

'Holy cow. I've had my first encounter with predatory females, and I'm supposed to be a priest.'

He was shaking all over.

'They used to be such harmless little girls. Who would have imagined it? I've known them since they were ten.'

He stayed wide awake and sharp all night; not the slightest difficulty. With every breath of wind he feared they were back. Just as well the Brigadier remained at home and didn't inspect twice, because the toffee stuck his jaws together and how would he have explained? For an hour at least he wondered if they'd ever unstick again.

And what of Kerry? Wasn't that a brute! Silly girl. Kerry with a crush on the Brigadier!

Eleven

(June 4, 1925 — October 16, 1938)

You get caught up in these things because you're born to them.

You get born to your very own destiny, like founding a nation or drowning at sea or being blinder than a blank brick wall with your glasses off.

You get born to going to church on Sundays.

You get born to frequenting the pubs and glugging down the beer and betting on the ponies come Saturday.

Well, it's true some appear to find their way to perdition unaided, but the exceptions prove the rule.

You get born to keeping watch on cliff-tops.

You get born into families that dive off the deep end for health or wealth or religion or politics or the great outdoors life, and you're stuck with it until you can pack your bag and skedaddle. Until then the sensible way to live with it, is to bend with it, is to join in, is to be the big brown-eyed kid about the place. Or you can become a continuing part of it by passive consent and inherit the family millions.

Whether you live in a mud-hut or a manor-house can be blamed upon the oddities of your birth and the company your parents keep, and who can say with certainty you had nothing to do with either?

For the same reason, you're given three meals a day or a few ounces of rice – or jackboots and taught how to goosestep – or a bat and taught to keep your eye on the ball. In each case, the life you get stuck with derives from destiny or the so-called accident of birth.

Hear my word, brethren, and mark it; accidents, as such, do not happen. There might be collisions, calamities or misfortunes, but all events happen because other events precede them. Even earthquake, flood, famine and meteor-strike.

So-called accidents catch you napping because they've been getting ready to happen and drop on you like blocks of concrete when you're not looking. But the all-powerful gods do not inflict this drastic kind of destiny upon helpless human beings in the way of small boys upending kettles of boiling water over ants. The accidents of life are more likely to be the result of one's own wish or one's own consent or one's own carelessness, though they may be the result of an evil presence like Herr Hitler or the diphtheria.

Take Hogan. When he set foot on Tangu Tangu he was sixteen years and seven weeks of age. Born June 4, 1925; sun sign Gemini, rising sign Pisces, Cancer moon. Well, you can't win 'em all.

Hogan Hanley Hancock, a nice name with nice rhythms to it, with good sounds, and why not? You've got to get something out of being human even if it's only a name with rhythms.

Hogan wore glasses. Such was his destiny.

Hogan had been wearing glasses since he was three. He caught the diphtheria and was lucky to get out of it still being Hogan in one compact piece. He got out of it with his eyesight in a kind of classic mess, and when other kids rushed out of doors to play football up and down King Edward Street, Hogan stopped inside with his glasses on to do his piano practice, or his homework, or to rearrange his stamp collection.

By the time he was eleven he had the biggest and most often rearranged stamp collection you ever heard of. Kids who lived down the far end of King Edward Street, about a hundred houses away, and hardly knew him, boasted of it. 'We got the best stamp collection in miles in our street. I seen it. He showed it to me, Hogan did, for three match box tops.'

King George V was rumoured to have the best stamp collection in the world. Hogan's came next.

Hogan got his stamps together by swapping everything he could lay hands on.

He swapped butterflies, iridescent green Christmas beetles, quartz chips from the disused quarry in King James Street where kids were not allowed, matchbox tops, answers to sums, green quinces and banana passionfruit in season, Laxettes that he didn't need for his constipation when the passionfruit was ripening, phonetic spelling lessons, cigarette cards, and so on.

Hogan was also top of his class and always won the prize. The prize for Dux. Not for coming second or anything. Not for making progress or anything. For King Pin. For the kid with the brains. He also won the Scripture Prize given by the lady from the Baptists, the Total Abstinence Prize given by the lady from the Women's Christian Temperance Union, the Best Essay Prize on 'My Visit to the Match Factory' given by the man from Bryant & May's, and the Sonata Prize given at Miss Ilya Crabtree's School of Pianoforte in Earl of Chatham Road.

A wonderful collection of books he had. All because he had to wear glasses.

Hogan also ran the King Edward Home Library out of the lock-up cupboard on the back porch, and on Saturday mornings at 9.30 showed movies in his bedroom for whatever you would offer in the way of admission, except promises. He used the Lion Brand made in Japan hand-cranked projector costing twelve shillings and sixpence that his parents gave him for Christmas, 1935, and the square of white wall next to the wardrobe, though usually no one came except his little sister Carrie because the films were always the same.

Hogan had dreams of owning a life-size library when he grew up, with books he didn't have to win. Next door to the library there'd be this grey building like a bank, with burglar-proof locks and alarm bells and plate-glass display cases housing his world-famous stamp collection. A hundred yards farther on, past his block of rented-out shops, he'd have this picture theatre built to look like the Bijou, with minarets, battlements, steeples, and a clock tower on the outside, and a dark blue ceiling with twinkling stars on the inside, along with genuine Axminster carpet, gold-painted Greek statues without any clothes on, and an ivory Wurlitzer that went up and down through a hole in the floor when you pressed a button.

Other times Hogan sat in the bay window at the front of his house, behind the net curtains, catching glimpses of the kids kicking the football up and down King Edward Street, and taking his glasses off and giving them a polish.

Then Hogan's Mum and Dad got religion. They caught it from the Griffithses who lived two doors up the street, the Griffithses always having been a bit that way inclined. The name of the religion was S.W.O.R.D.

This happened because Jon Griffiths had been slipping handbills about the coming end of the world into letterboxes up and down King Edward Street, earning himself threepence to buy hot potato cakes at the fish and chips shop. The handbills provoked some people to laughter and worried others half out of their minds.

The Griffithses were descended from generations of chapel people back in Wales and went to the Methodists on Sunday mornings and to S.W.O.R.D. on Sunday afternoons. The Hancocks being Church of England went to Holy Trinity to get married and to christen their children. Sometimes they went to the Annual Fête as well.

It was October, 1938, and Mr Chamberlain had not long flown back to Britain from Germany waving a famous piece of paper that might have been terribly important if Herr Hitler had been playing football with his kids up and down the Wilhelmstrasse, instead of training them to play Blitzkriegs up and down the North Sea coast.

Hogan hadn't been feeling notably nervous about Mr Chamberlain having to rush off to Germany to try to prevent the Battle of Armageddon. King Edward Street was five weeks by ship from Europe, even a couple of weeks by aeroplane, and that allowed Hogan plenty of time to be somewhere else, even at Quambertook with his Great Aunt Sophie, if Hitler started coming. Hogan being only thirteen and not able to find his glasses if they got moved without his permission, was not likely to be made into a soldier unless everybody else fell dead. Hogan reckoned this was the best bit of luck he'd had since the diphtheria.

Then his Mum and Dad got the religion.

Which only goes to show that nothing's sacred, Hogan said.

They got it suddenly, as if they had stepped out-of-doors to take the sun and a block of concrete had dropped on them.

There they were, that lovely Sunday afternoon, a nice family group taking a walk to the tram, paying their threepenny fares and getting off at the Bijou, not giving a thought to that great block of concrete whistling down through the clouds.

It was as if they were going to the pictures in broad daylight, though instead of posters out on the footpath to advertise the films, Union Jacks and Stars and Stripes and flags of Commonwealth countries were fluttering all around, and people outside were selling books about England and the Great Pyramid and God's Promises, and Mrs Griffiths, believe it or not, was giving away cups of tea free in the foyer. She even had tumblers of raspberry vinegar to give the kids. Hogan had two to make sure he wasn't dreaming. Inside everyone was singing songs about God of Our Fathers Known of Old and they were playing trumpets and trombones and huge brass boomers and talking about the end of the world which was due to happen at any moment.

So important they all looked on the stage. Brigadier Palmer sat centrally in the high-backed polished wood chair. He sat straight and square and had a jaw like one of the granite steps at Parliament House. When he stood up he was six-feet-ten inches tall.

'Glup,' said Hogan, for he was the tallest man Hogan had ever seen.

Mrs Victoria Alexandra Shuffle sat on the Brigadier's right. When she stood up full and firm at four-feet-ten inches in her flat-heeled English walking shoes, you had to look twice to make sure she wasn't still sitting. She wore a fluffy pink dress and a puffy pink hat and long pink gloves and shiny pink shoes and looked like the Queen.

'Is that the Queen?' Hogan hissed.

'Don't be stupid,' his mother said.

'Looks like the Queen,' Hogan hissed.

'It's not,' hissed his mother. 'The Queen's in England and you know it.'

Jeffrey Hawkins sat on the Brigadier's left. He owned a piece of Broken Hill Proprietary, drove a Bentley Eight Litre, and in 1935 flew a single-engined Lockheed from England to Australia in the Centenary Air Race.

'*That's Jeffrey Hawkins*,' Hogan hissed, his eyes making huge circles. 'Gawd, what do y'know about that!'

'Shhhh,' Hogan's mother hissed back.

Richard Cunningham sat in the next chair, on the Brigadier's left. The real Richard Cunningham. The one made out of flesh and blood instead of printer's ink and paper. It was like seeing God.

'It's the real Richard Cunningham,' Hogan hissed, feeling all peculiar, as if he was having a dream or something, as if he was about to wake up. 'I wish he was wearing his green hat.'

'Shhhh,' Hogan's mother hissed.

'All these famous people,' whispered Hogan, 'and a lady looking like the Queen as well.'

'Oh do be quiet, please,' pleaded Hogan's mother.

Hogan's Dad sat there looking like he'd just died but hadn't stopped twitching, because everyone knew he didn't go for religious stuff. Everyone knew he spent Sundays in his garden swearing at the damage wrought by snails and the district cats, and had come along only to be neighbourly. They knew because he told them. So sitting there looking as if he was suffering death pains

63

fitted the picture of his public image.

Poor fellow hadn't reckoned on getting squashed in his seat. He hadn't given that block of concrete a serious thought.

Twelve

(circa 1700 B.C. — October 16, 1938)

S.W.O.R.D. said it was international and interdenominational.

That's what it said. Straight out. Right away.

Its educational function was to interpret the mysteries that had come to separate God from Man. Its practical function was to intercede with God for all people and all faiths. Its ultimate function was to rescue the Chosen from the brink of oblivion.

Hogan couldn't remember half the words, and Hogan's father couldn't pronounce them, but everyone seemed to know what they meant.

S.W.O.R.D. said it was offering the truth of the world to the people of the world, no matter how shocking the truth had to be.

Anyone who heard the truth and ignored it had only himself to blame. To blame. To blame.

S.W.O.R.D. said if one had never heard the truth and so did nothing about it, everything would go on happening just the same. Tough luck. A universal law was operating, and like gravity it went on operating whether you knew about it or not. The university professor and the savage both broke their heads if they dived into the pool that wasn't deep enough.

'That's right,' Hogan said to himself.

Evil, said S.W.O.R.D., was about to consume itself and the world would perish in the fire.

In the fire, said S.W.O.R.D.

Real fire, said S.W.O.R.D.

65

We are not employing figures of speech.

'Gawd,' said Hogan to himself, 'and I'd been hoping that they were.'

Were you, said S.W.O.R.D., above the perils of the world? Could you order the sun not to set?

'No,' said Hogan, 'not me. I've tried. Went down just the same.'

Could you, said S.W.O.R.D., quell a volcano by command? Could you change your blood group by ordering it to obey your will?

No, said S.W.O.R.D. No. No.

'And they're dead right,' Hogan said to himself.

S.W.O.R.D. was for the Eternal Consciousness – a name they sometimes used for God – having lost patience; for having stood from the people of the world all he intended to stand, notably from the assorted 'children' of Gog, Magog, Ham, Cain, and other Biblically-named peoples who survived and populated the Earth to this day.

'That'd make them the oldest children alive,' Hogan said to himself. 'Children with wrinkles. Children with long white beards.'

S.W.O.R.D. can tell you, said S.W.O.R.D., who you are and what you are and where you came from. You might be surprised. Oh yes, friend, you might be surprised to discover you did not come from Vienna, as you have supposed, or from London, or from Dublin, or from Moscow or Copenhagen.

'I bloomin' well know I didn't,' Hogan said to himself. 'I came from St George's Hospital in Cotham Road.'

Don't, said S.W.O.R.D., imagine that what we say does not concern you. Tough luck if you thought it didn't. Your origins are as unchangeable as those of the person next door, transmitted to you from ancient times in your blood, in your seed.

'I'm no bloomin' thistle,' Hogan said to himself. 'I've got toes on me feet and hair on me head and a belly button in the middle.'

Your origins, said S.W.O.R.D., are impossible to erase, and they'll dog you to your grave, which, as we have said before, has drawn closer than you'd allowed yourself to hope.

'Is this what they call religion?' Hogan said to himself. 'It's like a horror movie.'

S.W.O.R.D. was for God having the big clean-up any day now with cataclysmic fire.

Fire, said S.W.O.R.D. Real fire. *We are not employing figures of speech.*

'There they go again,' Hogan said to himself, 'sayin' those awful things.'

S.W.O.R.D. wasn't for having a celebration about it. Oh no. S.W.O.R.D. wasn't whooping round the block shouting *Hooray Hooray.* S.W.O.R.D. didn't like the idea any more than you did. If S.W.O.R.D. grabbed a hot coal it got burnt the same as anyone else.

'I'm glad to hear it,' Hogan said to himself. 'I was beginning to wonder.'

Evil would generate the fire out of its weapons of war and God would allow the fire to burn.

To burn, said S.W.O.R.D., with real raging fire.

It scared the daylights out of Hogan, though his little sister Carrie didn't mind. She'd brought a Dutch baby doll to play with, which she kept undressing and holding out to toilet. And Hogan's Dad was sitting there like he'd turned to white stone. And Hogan's Mum was looking other ways all the time. When Hogan poked her in the side to attract her attention, she said, 'Ouch. Shhhh.'

S.W.O.R.D. went on to say that if you knew about their teachings, there was a possibility you might be delivered.

Delivered, said S.W.O.R.D. Do you hear us spell it out? Saved from the fire.

'I hear,' said Hogan to himself, 'and about blinkin' time, too.'

You'd not be delivered through any merit you might possess. Merit had nothing to do with it. God had laid down some rules for protection, for deliverance, for survival, and you might fit the rules. But if you didn't know what the rules were, you'd never be able to fit them, would you?

'All the time they go on being right,' Hogan said to himself.

God's laws operated like the laws of the country you lived in. Your ignorance of the laws of your country was not the fault of the law-makers, and was not a valid defence in Court. Your not knowing of God's laws was not God's fault either, and would not be a valid defence when you stood up to be judged.

'*Judged?*' Hogan said, almost out loud.

Things might be less complicated, said S.W.O.R.D., if you could trace your national blood line back to the ancient Hebrew peoples to whom God granted special privileges. This meant you had to identify the birthplace of your nation. You might get lucky and come up trumps. God extracted substantial promises from these ancient peoples in return for the privileges, so it was a contract, and it worked two ways like any other contract. You had to obey the conditions or the contract didn't operate.

The everlasting privileges that God offered were not offered to the Jews exclusively, as the world had supposed. The Jews were one blood line only of the peoples to whom the promises were made and had never claimed to be otherwise.

Praise God, said S.W.O.R.D., for being born Anglo-Saxon-Celtic.

'Hey?' Hogan said out loud.

Being born of Anglo-Saxon-Celtic stock, said S.W.O.R.D., is to stand squarely in the hereditary line. God's marvellous promises were offered to us!

'Gawd,' said Hogan out loud.

'Shhhh,' said his mother.

Praise God, said S.W.O.R.D., for His Mercy. We don't deserve it.

Voices called from here, there, and everywhere. 'Praise God. Hallelujah.'

But, said S.W.O.R.D., we have fulfilled our side of the bargain even less effectively than the Jews. Our promises are broken, dishonoured, forgotten, yet never in history have we stood at greater risk. An awful end looms over all of us, Jews and British and Americans alike, fire, real fire, and God cannot help unless we stand up and shout, '*We are your people. We remember our promises. Deliver us.*'

We might as well have been born German, said S.W.O.R.D.

The theatre hushed.

Yes, said S.W.O.R.D., for all the help that God can send while we so grossly disobey him, we might as well be German. To be German is the ultimate calamity.

'Poor Auntie Lizzie,' said Hogan. 'I hope God knows her name was Hancock before it was Schwartz.'

'Shhhh.'

Face the truth, said S.W.O.R.D., as it applies to you and to the nation of which you are a part. We shout to the world that being born to any nation that willingly allies itself to Germany is national and personal suicide. We shout the warning towards Rome, towards Tokyo, towards Moscow, towards Madrid – yea – even towards London and Washington and Mr Chamberlain's infamous piece of paper.

'I hope they're not shouting this way,' Hogan said to himself, 'or I'll be catching the next train to Quambertook to see me Auntie Sophie.'

Yet, said S.W.O.R.D., being born to either side is in your seed. It's in your origins. In some incomprehensible way it was always meant to be, though the seed has come down to you across thousands of years of which not a detail or a day can or ever could have been changed by you.

How, said S.W.O.R.D. can this be fair or reasonable or just? How can any person dictate the country of his birth or be responsible for what that country did or didn't do, now, or at any other time?

It has nothing to do with what is fair or reasonable or just, said S.W.O.R.D. You are what you are through immutable law. That means inevitable, unchanging, unavoidable. That means destiny.

S.W.O.R.D. did not make this so. S.W.O.R.D. tells you it is so. God's ways are not man's ways.

S.W.O.R.D. promises nothing, for S.W.O.R.D. is but human and prayer is its only power. S.W.O.R.D. is not saying join up with us and when the world burns you'll be safe and sound. To make declarations of the kind would debase us. We offer knowledge. We offer nothing more that we can be sure of.

We can tell you what is happening in the world and why it is happening and how you may be able to cope with it. We repeat, any day now the world must become a fire in which all flesh may be consumed. How could we as human beings wish this to be the fate of our world, or the fate of ourselves, or the fate of anyone else?

We love the ones who are dear to us, our families, our friends, our children. We love the beauty of our world, but S.W.O.R.D. says if there's an escape from it when it burns, we want to know about it.

The Bible tells us that if we live by God's laws as well as we are able, that if we know what God offers and ask Him for it, that if we believe God does not break His promises, a way of escape will appear. We will pass unburned through the fire. We will be lifted up to a safe place. We know not how. We know not where. It is miraculous and marvellous, but it is written in the Bible that it will be so. And all other flesh will be burned in the fire.

Real fire, said S.W.O.R.D.

We are not employing figures of speech.

Thirteen

(October 16, 1938)

It was a shattering afternoon in the Bijou.

Jolting home afterwards on the tram in the sunlight and the open air was like stepping back into pre-history.

It wasn't real out there in the open air. Everything you saw was existing in a kind of limbo. All the nice orderly houses and the nice orderly shops and the nice orderly people were about to turn into ashes. Nothing felt real except the consuming fire of destruction which was but a breath away.

'Strewth,' Hogan's poor old Dad said when they got to No. 69 King Edward Street. He scarcely even touched his hat to little Miss Finch in her garden across the road. Then he got his nose inside and shut the door as if pulling up the drawbridge to protect his family from demons and devils and savages and Nazis.

'Wasn't that just terrible,' he said. 'Wasn't that just awful.'

He flopped in the faded leather chair that Hogan's great-grandfather was suspected to have stolen in Ballarat in 1864 and started stroking the arm of it as if someone was about to take it off the heirloom list.

Hogan, though anxious to get back to his stamp collection to take his mind off everything else, stopped half-way down the passage to his room, half-way through a stride.

'All that proof, Phyllis,' his Dad was saying on the other side of the wall. 'All those dates and prophecies they dug up. Everything fitting together like they'd read it in yesterday's newspaper, instead of digging it up out of books and stones and scrolls thousands of years old.'

Hogan's Mum sounded lifeless. 'You don't believe it, do you, not seriously?'

'Well, don't you?'

Hogan, wobbling on one foot, waited for her to start laughing. She didn't. Instead, she went so quiet he could feel her silence through the wall. It made the nerves in his neck and shoulders tingle. It made him sore.

Carrie, who was six, said, 'Can I have an Anzac out of the jar?'

Hogan's Mum's home-made Anzacs were crisp sticky biscuits made with quantities of golden syrup.

Carrie got ignored.

Hogan's Dad said, 'I only went to be polite. I only went to be neighbourly. I think I only went for the giggle. But these people know what they're talking about, Phyllis. They're real responsible people. I reckoned they'd be a bunch of ratbags, though now I come to think of it you could never call Griffiths a ratbag. He was very good to you that time I broke me leg.'

'They make you wonder, don't they, why we ever bothered to have children?'

'Can I have an Anzac out of the jar?'

Hogan settled on two feet. Did they mean what he thought they meant by bothering to have children?

'That fellow who did the speaking is the Member of Parliament, Phyllis. Well, I guess I knew that, but did you get an eyeful of the height of him? He must be damn near seven feet tall. I was expecting him to be the brigadier of some boys' brigade. Not the hero. Not the real one. Always thought of them as different people. And Jeff Hawkins was on the platform. Did you see him? And Richard Cunningham, the test cricketer. A down-to-earth cussing fellow like Cunningham. And they were saying Chamberlain's piece of paper isn't worth tuppence! That it's a sell-out. That it's drawing up a contract with the Devil. My gawd, Phyllis, what sort of days are we livin' in?'

'I'm having an Anzac out of the jar.'

'I'm real shook-up,' Hogan's Dad said. 'Can they be right? All this fire, Phyllis. If that's the way it's to be, so soon, what do we do about it? Do we make decisions? This being taken up bodily from the Earth and removed by God to a safe place – simply by knowing and believing it can be done. Strike me, why not? He made the Universe. Doing a little thing like snatching people up to a safe place would be dead easy. Snatching us up in an instant from the street or wherever we are. Where is the safe place, for gawd's sake? In the clouds? On the moon? They might be right about this fire, really right. You've only got to look at the world. It's all there waiting to happen. But this getting snatched and being saved from it all. I don't feel worthy, Phyllis. I mean, what am I? You know me. What terrible days they are.'

Hogan went to his own small room and sat on his bed.

He had always known his daydreams were stupid.

It would have been better to have died in 1928 when he had the diphtheria, and had been too young to know about it and too young to care about it and wouldn't have known whether he was alive or dead.

Hogan was still sitting on his bed an hour later, tapping his right middle finger into the hollow under his right knee, when his mother called him for Sunday-night tea and cakes.

She baked the cakes on Saturday mornings in a wood-fire stove to her very own recipes. She was a genius. Hogan's Dad reckoned she was more than any of them deserved.

Cornish egg and parsley patties. Lamingtons. Napoleons. Gingerbreads. Shortbreads. Nutbreads. Brownies. Anzacs. Cheesies. Macaroons. Coconut Kisses. Butterfly Creams. Great-Grandmothers. And good old Chortle Chumley's Chewy Chocolate Crumbles.

She could add up, too.

Fourteen

(August 22, 1941 — December 6, 1941)

There was Jon on his cliff, week following week following week, fighting his night-time battles against sleep and mosquitoes. He was sure he should have become immune to both. It was like a permanent case of the sleepless measles. Maybe the itching and the scratching kept him awake.

Sometimes he fought the battles in good heart, poking fun at everything, even at God for having created such a mess for humans to live in and then for having expressed the opinion on the very first page of the Bible 'that it was good'. Though Jon usually ended with an apology. 'I didn't really mean it. It's just that they expect me to stay awake up here getting eaten alive until goodness knows when, and I want to go to sleep at night under a mosquito net same as other people, the way you meant I should.'

Sometimes he fought the battle with an ache and a loneliness for Kerry. He had had aches about Kerry since she was twelve. Now she was going on seventeen. Now she was getting more and more gorgeous all the time, though he glimpsed her only once a week when he went into camp for the Sabbath Day Celebration Dinner.

'What did you make her so beautiful for? You should've made her horrible like the rest of them. Watch 'em turn thirteen, and urrgh. Like you'd knocked off for a coffee break for a few years, or something. Like you hadn't noticed what a sight they were becoming until it was almost too late to fix it. A real smart way of protecting little girls from boys. I reckon. Look at the MacWhorters.

74

Safe as houses.'

Sometimes he'd hear the horrible twins coming and he'd start sweating and swearing. They were a bigger pain than too many bananas.

'You'll get us caught! They'll think we're up to hanky-pankies!'

'We're not though, are we? Worse luck.'

Sometimes they wouldn't turn up for a week and getting through to dawn without them, even for a single night, was like winning a prize you'd never reckoned on. But they hung over everything like the chop. As if he didn't have enough to worry about. He was going grey, he was sure. He was sure he was the haggardest-looking kid anyone ever saw.

'*Get lost, you two!*'

But talking to those girls was like talking to a couple of trees.

'The Brigadier'll come back. He'll catch us.'

But the Brigadier never arrived while they were there and they never came before the Brigadier had been and gone.

Sometimes they brought news. He wondered where they got the news from, because he was sure they didn't hear it from Jeffrey Hawkins at the regular after-lunch session. Did they spend their lives eavesdropping? Did they have a secret tunnel under the Brigadier's hut?

He started thinking of them as the MacWhorter Sisters Detective Agency, but still didn't know who was who or which was which, unless one said, 'She's Phoebe, I'm Jessie.' Or the other said, 'She's Jessie, I'm Phoebe. She's nothing like me. Are you simple or something?'

They were terrible people. They did it on purpose, he was sure. He reckoned they shuffled their clothes and their names back and forth. He reckoned they were *interchangeable*.

One night they said, 'The Brigadier's getting worried about the Japanese. Everyone's reckoning the Operation's been set up in the wrong place. What'll happen to us if the Japanese come? We're helpless young girls. Will you protect us?'

'It's the Japanese that'll need protection.'

'We thought you were a gentleman,' said Jessie or Phoebe.

'Doesn't your mother care where you are? Doesn't she ever check up? Is she always out walking with Mr Tregellas? Why don't you pester Hogan instead?'

'Hogan's only a boy!'

'He's a year older than you are!'

'We like mature men. We don't go for kids.'

'Go away,' groaned Jon.

'The Brigadier's all upset about the Japanese because he's been hearing things on the wireless. He's been hearing that the Japanese are coming into the war. He's been sitting in his hut, looking worried, with his headphones on.'

'How do you know what he's hearing with his headphones on?'

'He's worried about the Japanese putting a spoke in our wheel. If the Japanese come, what'll happen to Operation Sword? They're not likely to let us go on with it, are they?'

'No,' said Jon.

'The brigadier keeps sending signals on the Morse Code. Tappedy-tap. The Brigadier keeps calling Australia and Australia doesn't answer. He keeps calling Rabaul and Rabaul doesn't answer. He's even tried the Philippines. Mr Hawkins reckons the transmitter wouldn't lift your hat off. He reckons the government gave us a brummy set because they never wanted to hear from us again. It can get the signals coming in, but can't send them out. Mr McBride's spent hours, spent days, trying to fix it. He just goes on shaking his head. And the ship was supposed to come back, too, wasn't it? And did it? Not on your life. Just as well we can grow lots to eat. Mr Cunningham reckons the ship's sunk. Reckons it never got back to Australia. Reckons how could a ship making all that smoke hope to get anywhere safely with a war going on? What with all the submarines and all the battleships.'

'Oh, go away,' cried Jon.

'Mr Tregellas reckons the Japanese'll come south. Not much good going north, hey? Only the polar bears up there. If they come south, Mr Tregellas says, we're right in the path, sitting up like Aunt Sallies at the fairground waiting to have our heads knocked off. All isolated. All on our own. What've we got to protect ourselves with? Two shotguns and four twenty-two's. And a ten-foot dinghy to make our escape in.'

'No doubt about you two. You're a real cheer-up society.'

'A hundred people to fit in the dinghy. A hundred and one probably. Mrs McBride's getting awful stout again. Who's going to sit in the dinghy? We bet it won't be us. Women and children first. You watch. And they'll tell us we're not children. And they'll tell us we're not women. Who's going to swim behind? One guess. Us. With all those sharks. Mr Hancock and Mr Oliver reckon we ought to be making outrigger canoes. No one's ever seen an outrigger canoe. Mr Oliver's going back to the drawing board to invent one. What's going to happen to us if the Japanese get here before the Heroes?'

'What heroes?'

'The Heroes of Light.'

'Grief,' said Jon.

'What do you mean by that?' said Jessie or Phoebe.

'I mean you should be looking for a nice deep hole to dive into.'

Fifteen

(August 22, 1941 — December 6, 1941)

'I'm going to marry Jon,' Phoebe said. 'He's beautiful.'

'What about me?' said Jessie.

'I don't want to marry you. You're my twin. You're a girl.'

'You know what I mean,' said Jessie. 'I'm the one that's going to marry Jon.'

'You're not, you know. You can visit on Sundays for afternoon tea and sit on the other side of the room.'

'Do I hear my loving sister talking?'

'Yup,' said Phoebe.

'I don't go for that,' said Jessie. 'Maybe we can come to an arrangement. Alternate days? Or week about?'

'We could toss a coin,' said Phoebe. 'Heads I win. Tails you lose.'

'This is going to be a problem, I think,' Jessie said.

'Don't see a problem,' said Phoebe. 'You can have Hogan.'

'And a pig's ear!'

'His Mum thinks he's marvellous.'

'If I'd had a baby like him,' said Jessie, 'I'd have drowned him.'

'Have Richard then.'

'Richard's ten!'

'Won't be ten forever, will he?'

'I'm not having Richard.'

'Have Alan then.'

'He's seven!'

'You're being difficult,' said Phoebe. 'All these beautiful boys and you're turning them all down.'

'But they're still crawling round their playpens! Would you want to get married to a little boy who'd rather cuddle his teddy bear?'

'I wouldn't know. I'm marrying Jon. Yum.'

Jessie and Phoebe based their movements about the island upon speed, deception and common sense. They explored their routes and memorized them. Then disguised them. One minute they might be dawdling along the sand in full view, the next, out of sight, they'd be heading with purpose through the jungle for their objective, though at night they moved with a proper degree of anxiety. Off their regular tracks the island was dark, dense, and confusing. And little wild pigs had big savage fathers. Once at around midnight they lost the way home, but kept their heads, took a few deep breaths, and tracked by sound and instinct for the beach. They were not in bed until 4 a.m. and no one seemed to notice they bore more scratches than usual.

In daylight they wore green cotton frocks with a leafy pattern of brown and yellow, worn threadbare, to the exasperation of their mother. 'Why must you go on irritating me like this? Pretty dresses you've hardly worn at all, dresses, dresses everywhere, yet off you go in rags. I've made gowns for Mrs Shuffle. I've made skirts for the Brigadier's aunt. Am I a common seamstress? I refuse to mend these rags one more time. I'll burn them. I'll bury them.'

'If,' said Jessie, 'you bury or burn our very favourite greenies, we'll take steps.'

'What do you mean by that?'

'Steps,' said Phoebe, with a grin from ear to ear, 'in pursuit of you and Mr Tregellas.'

'You're impertinent!'

At night they wore their old school uniforms, navy blue, which were just as heavily darned and just as badly worn.

'Pair of scruffs,' Mrs MacWhorter said irately. 'You shame me.'

79

Night or day they'd set out in careless fashion along the beach, heading away from the approaches to the cliff. In a couple of hours there they'd be again, coming back, bearing seashells or orchids or fruit or driftwood or interesting stones.

There wasn't a hut more like a magpie nest on Tangu Tangu. From time to time Mrs MacWhorter started throwing things hysterically, and there'd be a big clean-up, with Jessie and Phoebe ducking and dodging and wailing, 'Fair go, Mum. Fair go, Mum.'

Sometimes they came back from their travels wet to the skin. Once they returned uncommonly pale and shaken and both were sick for most of the night.

Jeff Hawkins called them Stanley and Livingstone.

Mrs Shuffle said, 'Can't say I'm keen you should be so far out of sight so often. Take care, girls.'

Mr Chambers said, 'You should arrange some group hikes. Would you like me to suggest it to the Brigadier?'

But no one, it seemed, gave really serious thought to them, any more than anyone gave thought, beyond appreciation, to Mr Cunningham at cricket with the children on the sand, or to Christopher McBride at the organ in the meeting hall, or to the stylish touches of ornamentation the Misses Littlejohn gave their hut – for all was done during 'Family Free Time.'

Visit after visit to Jon they came away from the cliff-top like mice in a garden full of cats. They knew they must not underestimate the Brigadier.

Sixteen

(December 10, 1941)

Jessie and Phoebe were down to level ground, about a third of a mile from the booth where Jon sheltered from a sharp shower of rain, about three hundred yards from the sentry hut where Hogan slept, in the belt of dense growth which lay between the vegetables garden and the sea.

They had no warning. Suddenly, they clenched each other. Suddenly, they heard the voice.

'The nocturnals!'

There he was in the rain. Vague. Huge.

The instinct was to flee.

It was like walking into a wall not suspected to be there.

'Good evening, Phoebe. Good evening, Jessie.'

There wasn't a sound they could make, except noises of dismay.

The Brigadier said, 'Let's take a walk. Along the beach. I have no doubt you can get me there directly, hail, rain, or shine.'

'Sir. / .'

'The beach,' he said.

'Oh, crumbs,' moaned Jessie and Phoebe, sharing the thought and the word. Then Jessie thought, 'That's torn it. Has it ever.' And Phoebe thought, 'Mum'll kill us, I bet.' And Jessie thought, 'Lord, have mercy upon us, miserable offenders.' And Phoebe thought, 'It's awful awful. The disgrace.' And Jessie thought, 'He won't let us see Jon now. What'll we do if we can't see Jon any more? I'll die if I can't see Jon any more. Oh, we're caught, we're caught, it's awful to be caught.'

The Brigadier said, 'The beach.'

'It's wet,' said Phoebe, very short of breath.

'It's raining,' said Jessie dismally.

'The beach,' said the Brigadier.

'It's dark,' mumbled Phoebe. 'We can't see.'

'It's dark,' said Jessie with a sob. 'And there are prickly things and wild pigs.'

'The beach,' said the Brigadier.

They came down to hard sand over which high water had swept not long before.

Away he walked, legs as long as stilts. Keeping up with him was a scramble, a humiliation. Away he walked. And the rain swept on, and the clouds swept on, and stars came out. A million lights. Ten million lights. All those stars looking down. Every one a Hero.

Jessie and Phoebe were crying.

He said, 'You take me for an idiot. You imagine you deceive me with green by day and navy by night? Godfathers, I was designing camouflage for men and machines before you children were born. I've concealed a battalion on an open hillside.'

'Oh, please, sir.'

'Haven't I made allowances for your age and the romantic state of your minds? Haven't I understood your need to see the poor boy? I've not stopped you and you've visited him many times. I've allowed you to go wherever you've wished, even though you've broken promises and caused my lad up there much anxiety, I'm sure. Enough anxiety, perhaps, to keep him wide awake!'

'Please, sir. Please, sir.'

'No young person but yourselves has broken curfew. You've broken it five times. *On one occasion by four hours. What the hell were you doing all night through?*'

'We were lost. . .'

'If I had a guard-house I'd slap you in it on bread and water. To be *lost* is unforgiveable.'

'Oh, please, sir.'

'*Sir* be damned. You don't feel respect for me. It's a

82

reflex. It's a hiccough. You treat me like a joke.'

'We don't, we don't, we don't.'

'All this backing and forthing. All this to-ing and fro-ing. All this lying doggo in the thickets as I ride past. All this scaling of cliffs. All this slithering about the place like weasels.'

'We're not weasels. . .'

'Stop your snivelling. Great big hulking girls. You're almost sixteen years of age.'

He swung, almost collided with them, and went striding back, Jessie and Phoebe stumbling after.

'You know what's happened in the world in the last few days? Thought it through, have you? Got it all worked out? The Japanese are in the war. Outwitting generals and admirals. Won more battles in a couple of days than we've won in a couple of years. You reckon you can do better than generals and admirals?'

They whimpered wordlessly.

'The Japs can put a raiding party ashore at the other end of this island any night they please, and who'll know? This island is *strategic*. Flatten a mile of jungle or straighten out the grasslands and turn it into airstrips. Turn it into depots. You mark my word; you watch it happen. Am I to post sentries from hillock to hillock and shore to shore? Where do I get them? How do I link communications without a signal corps? Am I to deploy twenty-nine unarmed men and fourteen little boys to defend forty-four square miles and fifty-seven females? Lord, we'd never know the Japs were here until you two fools were found a couple of miles from camp with your throats cut.'

He turned on them. They were terrified. They thought he was about to strike them down.

'From now on, we set camp guards at night, guards with guns, demanding passwords, so your prancings and dancings are over.'

He passed through them, heading down the beach again. They followed, dazed.

'Breathe a word of this conversation and you'll find

83

yourselves on the mat. Publicly! Make no mistake, my ladies of the night. Fifteen years of age! Creeping round in the dark seeing boys!'

They could barely keep up with him. It was awful, awful. They were almost running – and almost too weak.

'But for a couple of tangle-footed teenagers you're not bad. Two hulking great girls melting into the earth like lumps of hot lard. Let's hope the fight for survival exploits and refines the instinct.'

He stopped, and they blundered into him, sobbing.

'Pull yourselves together. Let me see it happen. Instantly. Instantly. Come along.'

'I'll be good,' sobbed Phoebe, and everything folded beneath her. She buckled onto the wet sand and Jessie fell with her.

There he stood in the starlight like a monument, not moving.

He waited, and in a short time they rose towards him, as if assisted. Afterwards, they wondered about it.

'Survival,' he said.

In a while he repeated himself. 'Survival. What's it to me? Not much. What's it to you? At fifteen, at fifteen, just about everything. Poor little devils. Scarcely taken a bite of the apple. Mrs Shuffle says you can draw, that you both have a nice sense of perspective. You're excused school lessons as from tomorrow. Mrs Shuffle will not be expecting you any more. Each day, excluding the Sabbath, you'll take an ample lunch, a compass, and sketch pads, and you'll produce working maps for me, the terrain fully described, landmarks positioned, tracks assessed as good, fair or bad, and everything else or anything else that may assist us to survive a Japanese attack. I demand of you an effort beyond your physical strength. You'll be using will-power, just as my boys on the cliff have to use will-power to remain awake and alert. But like them, you'll be fed special rations to fuel the body, for a performance far beyond the normal call of duty is required of you. You will be escorted by two armed men, Mr Griffiths and Mr Hancock. Any questions?'

They were stunned.

'No questions? Well, I have one. Some weeks ago you came home stressed and ill. Why?'

He waited for their reply. Phoebe said, 'We found a cave. Under the cliff. The only way in is to swim. We tried three or four times. It was dangerous. It was about as wide as a room but went farther back. There was a little beach. There were bones. There were bones all over the place. They were human bones, sir. There were skulls.'

After a while, he said, 'Go home to bed and get some rest. Use the night for sleeping and see your boy friend on Sundays. Nothing shall be said. Nothing by me and nothing by you. We'll all keep our traps shut.'

Seventeen

(December 25, 1941)

'Here I sit,' said Jon to Hogan on Christmas night, though Hogan wasn't there. 'Having a real happy Christmas. A hunk of Christmas pudding in me supper and a nice fit of the twitch. Everyone sound asleep down there in their cosy little cots snoring their silly heads off. You snoring your head off. All of you having happy believings, same as usual. All this mumbo-jumbo, all this praying about the Heroes of Light, with the Japanese carving everything up into little bits. I don't know how you go on believing it, Hogan. Lucky dog, lucky you, believing all this stuff, sleeping down there in your little cot. I reckon the Government should send a warship and take us off. If they don't, the Japs will. I bet you the Japs have got a headstone ready and waiting. *Here lies S.W.O.R.D. Kaput.*'

Talking to Hogan when Hogan wasn't there was the only way Jon *could* talk to him. All their lives, living only two houses apart in King Edward Street, they'd looked at each other and mumbled.

'It's not my fault, Hogan. I didn't make my own brain, did I? I came alive and there it was. I can't stop it from thinking. Every day it thinks louder and louder.'

Jon spent time talking to the Brigadier, too. In the absence of the Brigadier!

'Now look here, sir, I've been your faithful servant. I've been stuck up here for months. What *are* these Heroes? What am I waiting for?'

The only time he asked the Brigadier point-blank, he got a shake of the head, as if the Brigadier wished he'd go away.

Mrs Shuffle, Executive Secretary of S.W.O.R.D., didn't know either. 'An idle question, lad.'

So *what* was coming?

Archangels?

Dragons with spread wings?

Half-human creatures lit up like candles, with heads like gods?

Or some unimaginable Heavenly fleet of inconceivable vessels of incomparable majesty coming in a brilliance of light that blinded you?

The words you had to use to frame the thought were daunting enough. Could you keep your feet on solid earth and think it through? Yet these apparently sane people, several of some note in the world, were inviting God to appear, physically, visibly, with muscle. Oh wow. Oh wow-eeee.

Every day they prayed it, their hands upon the heads of the children.

You could hear them praying it beside their beds, praying it in the meeting hall, praying it over their dinners, praying it out in the open, raising it to the skies.

Well, it used to be that ideas like God's presence in the world meant the spirit or the imagination.

What if these prayers called up evil forces worse than those already savaging the Earth? Myth and legend warned people against inviting the gods out of their palaces. Myth and legend might have been racial memories of the most God-awful disasters.

The Brigadier wasn't the only giant in Jon's life. His Headmaster at the Grammar School was the other.

To all things there was an up and a down, his Headmaster said, a back and a front, a right and a wrong, an outside and an inside. Where one existed the other existed also.

Ideas like it had engrossed the human mind since humans started waking up to themselves. If you admitted the existence of Good, you had to admit the existence of Evil, though you could call them X or Y, Positive or

Negative, God or the Devil, whatever you fancied. If one side could poke its nose into human affairs, the other side could also.

His Headmaster said, 'Don't allow your learning or the cold clear air of morning to take the edge off what you feel in your bones. I'm saying to you, boy, don't believe everything you read or hear just because the voice of authority utters it.

'Now what idiot would willingly stand around while God or the Devil arrived on his personal square foot of earth? If that's the object of this absurd expedition, I wish I had the power to stop you – or to influence your parents against it. The Brigadier should be put away as a public menace.'

'Okay,' said Jon to Hogan, when Hogan wasn't there, 'let's say the Brigadier's right. Wouldn't it be better to be dead now than alive in the middle of such magnitudes of good or evil? Give it some thought, Hogan. You're supposed to be a real bright kid. Didn't all that stuff come to an end when they stopped writing the Bible? Wasn't that why they stopped writing the Bible, there being nothing new to put down? Or is this Doomsday Book of the Brigadier's the journal of a modern prophet? In ages to come will his book stand beside the others? *The Book of Doomsday According to Palmer.*

'Yeh,' said Jon to the bright black sky, 'but who really expects events like it to happen? These great last battles of good and evil, the Armageddons, and the marvellous Milleniums to come after? Who expects them *intellectually*, except the people who try to bring them about – the Caesars and the Hitlers and the prophets and the starry-eyed disciples like us who follow?

'Yeh,' said Jon, directly to himself upon the cliff, 'you can stand off and see that it's stupid. But if you're on the spot you get caught up in it like all those Germans screaming Hitler's name. It's the same madness.

'Oh, brother,' said Jon Griffiths to Jon Griffiths, 'the excitement of it at the start. As if ordinary people using their ordinary human powers could *stop* Hitler!

88

'The Brigadier reckons that belief's to be found in your bones, put there by God. Exactly what my Headmaster says to prove the opposite opinion!'

Yeh. And in private the Brigadier had said to Jon, 'I trust you above all others to remain awake. You're the one. But by God if you fail to see their coming, if you fail to raise the alarm –'

Made Jon feel like fail and the world drops dead. Like turn yourself into Atlas, boy, and carry the world on your back.

Already he was saying to himself, 'I'm doing what because of that Brigadier? Stayin' awake while everyone else sleeps. For how long am I to go sitting on the brink of this cliff waiting for the end of the world?'

Eighteen

(January 1, 1942)

Each day, with the sunrise, or soon after, up came the day-watch in person, wandering into view, up the long slant of the approaches to the cliff, chewing on a hunk of grey bread.

Hogan would be barefoot, more often than not, having lost his sandals somewhere, probably under his nose. He'd be half-buttoned up with his shirt hanging out.

'Hi, Jon.'

'Hi, Hogan.'

Sometimes they managed more.

'Nothing to report, Jon?'

'Of course there's not.'

'Don't bite me head off, mate, Why say it like that?'

'Well you'd have known, wouldn't you? You'd have got called in the night. Everyone would've been running all over the place.'

Sometimes they took the conversation other ways.

'I don't know, I don't know, I don't know.'

'You don't know what, Hogan?'

'I don't know.'

The girls were right. He was hopeless.

Hogan had been known to say, 'I reckon the Brigadier. . .I reckon the Brigadier. . .'

'You reckon the Brigadier what?'

'I reckon.'

Another time Hogan said, 'Staying awake in the sun up here, on your own, not even allowed to read a book. . .Take my word for it. . . What's wrong with everybody else? Sitting up here in broad daylight like a pimple on a pyramid, nothing to do, nowhere to go, month in, month out. . .'

'Sitting up here all night's not much of a laugh either.'

'Yeh.'

'Yeh.'

'I saw sharks,' Hogan said on New Year's Day, 1942, after the Japanese were charging like warhorses in all directions. 'I counted twenty-two sharks. One was flying the Rising Sun. One was flying the Swastika.'

'You've got to be kidding.'

'Yeh.'

Jon was glad they didn't spend more time together. Hogan was beginning to worry him.

They sat in a kind of booth, four posts squared six feet apart, a thatch of palm leaves over the top more or less keeping off the rain unless it drove in hard from the sea.

Every now and then Jon found himself thinking about the prophet Jonah in the olden days sitting in his booth outside the wicked Syrian city of Nineveh. Sitting there because God told him to. God even arranged for a nice shady vine to grow over Jonah's booth to keep off the sun and the rain. Lucky Jonah.

Jonah was the fellow who'd been swallowed by the fish and he'd had a few complaints to make about it at the time. Jon reckoned he'd have made a few complaints about it, too.

There was old Jonah, looking forward very much to the day when God would destroy Nineveh in the midst of some awful disaster, because Jonah couldn't stand Syrians.

A hundred and twenty thousand children lived in Nineveh in those days, along with all the grown-ups, and all the cows and sheep and horses and goats and cats and dogs and white rabbits in hutches and butterflies and beetles and worms.

Jonah sat there waiting for the big bang, rubbing his hands together.

God didn't come. A cheeky little cutworm came instead

and nibbled through the main stem of Jonah's shady vine, and there was old Jonah left out in the sun, fainting from the heat, and the Syrians got let off with a caution.

The more thought Jon gave to it, the more it seemed that sitting in a booth on a cliff at Tangu Tangu waiting for God to fry the world, and sitting in a booth outside Nineveh waiting for a big bang, were the same thing. But could you swim three thousand miles home? You'd end up down a fish's throat yourself!

Back home, what next? Next you'd be in the army quicker than you could say Jack Robinson.

Well, if you'd got born and hadn't died of the infantile paralysis or something, you kept on getting closer to being eighteen every day. Then they'd stand you against the wall and shoot you.

Eighteen years come March 15, 1942!

Soon the Brigadier would be whistling up a passing war canoe. 'Taxi! Taxi!'

Then the Brigadier would say to the captain of the war canoe, 'This kid, he's ripe and ready. You take this kid to the boss man in Rabaul. This kid is beautiful gun fodder. You bring me back a receipt from the boss man and I'll pay you one pith helmet and one pair of regulation army shorts and you'll be the sartorial sensation of the South Seas.'

'It's a lousy prospect,' Jon said to Hogan, Hogan being sound asleep in the sentry hut several hundred yards away at the time, 'though it's different for you, lucky beggar, being blinder than the blunt end of a blanket. I'm the one that's got to get meself blown to bits. How'd you like that hanging over you night and day? And the only girls on offer round here are Jessie and Phoebe, Kerry the Berry bein' all dedicated to the vision splendid. The war over there and Jessie and Phoebe over here!

'Isn't it a fellow's right to have a couple of years for growing, for doing a whoop, for not adding up the cost of every breath you breathe? It's all in this book. I'd have brought it if they'd have let me. 'You don't want that stuff,' they said. 'That's profane. Where did you get it from, Jon Griffiths? From your Headmaster? Along with *Jurgen*? God forgive him.'

'The book says you've got to have your interlude of *joie de vivre*. I like the sound of that. A year or two of knowing what it feels like to be turning into a man without having to act all grown-up.

'The book says that growing time's your birthright. Otherwise why go through all the agony to get started?

'I find it discouraging, Hogan, from my position, my position being different from your position, you being in the happy position of being blinder than the blank end of a blunt instrument, and in no danger whatsoever of being turned into anything military. *Discouraging*, Hogan, knowing about this war and about getting done over good and permanent in it. But how do you stop knowing it?

'It's like the Tree of Knowledge, the book says. Once you know that life's not a great big rosy apple, all you've got left is knowing about it.

'The fool climbs the Everests, the book says, because the Everests are there. The wise man stands off at a distance and dreams his dreams.

'Back home, Hogan, I heard kids say they couldn't wait to turn eighteen to get stuck into this war. I aim on stayin' seventeen for ever.

'I mean, until you're eighteen who's pushing you except those hatchet-faced femmes who stop you in the street? Why aren't you in the army, young man? Got a yellow streak?

'The shrews.

'But the day you turn eighteen they're all at it. The Government's at it. Your Auntie Florrie's at it. Your Mum and Dad are at it.

'Out you go, kid, and be a hero. Fight for freedom. Fight for your King. Fight for the right. Win your glory.

'What they mean is, better you than us, kid.

'At midnight the day turns over and there you are. Time to put eighteen candles on the cake. Time to sing, *Why was he born so beautiful, why was he born at all?*

'My trouble, Hogan, is the sitting up here all night

while everyone else sleeps in their cosy little cots. Sitting up here waiting for my end or the world's end. Same difference, I reckon. Waiting for God to come and start up the millenium. Imagine the millenium! If God's like what some of them say, who'd want it?

'Take a minute off, Hogan. Look around. The God who made this Universe has got more on his mind than laying down a few do's and don't's to make life difficult for humans. He's got fire pulsing through his veins. He'd scare the Holy Joes out of their wits. He scares me, I'm tellin' you.'

Nineteen

(January 3, 1942)

Kerry's appointment with the Brigadier was for 11.45, her only private meeting with him, ever. She made the appointment days in advance, hoping for an hour. Clearly, he thought fifteen minutes would do for a sixteen-year-old girl. He'd put her off before. That was the way of it.

The Brigadier's hour for interviews ended at noon.

'Yes, Kerry,' he said.

He glanced at her, as he'd often glanced up as she'd passed by, and looked back to his table again, to the open page. The pen in his fingers started moving like a slow metronome, as if he would prefer to be writing his lecture for Sunday, as if she were using up his time.

Kerry's pulse was much more rapid than the pen, the metronome, taking her breath.

The door of the hut was open. The shutters were propped up. Any gust of wind could have scattered every sheet of paper in the place, but the air barely moved. Even the sea was subdued. Only Kerry lived the storm.

She feared she might not be able to produce a word – that her voice might fail. It would have been better to have stayed away. To have gone on as before, alone. Nerves shook her lower jaw.

Small beads of sweat were forming on his face and on the bareness of his arms. Perhaps they'd remain until they troubled him, or streaked the page. Then he'd reach for a handkerchief, as she'd often seen him do, from a distance, night and day. He glanced up, then down again to the page.

'Don't stand, my dear.'

She wished recklessly to shut the door. She wished recklessly to drop the shutters, to take out the props. She wished recklessly for a few private minutes with him, out of her whole life.

Why should every moment be shared with crowds?

Then she'd say, 'My love for you now is not a little girl's. Don't you know?'

In her mind she shut the door and dropped the shutters, but the image turned to shame. A fantasy image, selfish, stupid.

She took the simple chair opposite him and the door remained open and the shutters remained up and everyone who had the inclination was free to walk by, to observe her, to say, 'What's Kerry done, all forlorn? Is he tearing a strip off her?'

Her hands dropped in resignation to her lap; the fantasy gone like a glow from a glass shattered with a stone.

How could she look up?

Her breath and pulse and nerves hurt like pains.

What was he writing? Was the pen not moving?

What was he thinking? His thoughts were silent.

What would he say? He uttered not a word.

She forced herself to raise her eyes. It was a humiliation.

He was watching her.

Wretchedly, she looked immediately another way, then back to her lap. Her clasped hands were clammy and white with strain.

A sigh came and Kerry wasn't sure whether it came from herself or from the other side of the table.

She wished he'd speak. She wished he'd help her. She wished he'd say, 'If you've changed your mind, Kerry, about seeing me, you may go.' She wished to be back in the schoolroom supervising the small children. The wishes came to nothing.

She struggled to put thoughts together, to project **an** audible voice. 'You haven't given me a special job like the others. Are all the teenagers important to you except me?'

Then she was not sure if she had asked the question in a logical manner, or made a question of it, or produced the sound.

She glanced up to appeal, to beg, but his eyes were down, as if quickly dipped, and he looked worried, looked concerned, and the point of his pen trembled against the open page.

Well, perhaps he didn't look worried. Perhaps he was thinking. Perhaps he had forgotten to a large extent that she was there. Perhaps the pen hesitated only over a word.

'The others have got special jobs.'

She had no doubt the words were spoken, as clearly, as plaintively, as anyone could express anything through clenched teeth.

He made no response.

Inside she said, 'Please, sir. Oh, please. I've loved you since I was a little girl. I let my father go to hold to you. Can't you give me any special care?'

In a while, the Brigadier said, 'I am aware of these matters.'

The school-bell rang for noon. She couldn't believe the time had gone.

She sought out his eyes with desperation. She wanted to say, 'Aware of what matters? Tell me. Tell me.'

His eyes were blue, were pale, were sad. 'That's it, Kerry.'

He smiled, and she had to walk away, tears overwhelming her.

Twenty

(October 16, 1938 — February 16, 1942)

Hogan was awake again; wide, wide awake again; and everything was changing key – the life like a fantasy that he lived day by day, the hard bunk in the sentry hut where he slept, the ritual, the routine, the discipline, the waiting, the eternal presence of the sea.

Everything felt threatened.

Suddenly everything felt dangerously real. Immediately real. Urgently real.

'Something's on,' he said aloud, sitting up in bed. 'I hope it's not the Japanese.'

For a moment he was wondering whether he would rather have faced the end of the world than the small silent men who wore spectacles into battle, thus endangering a principle.

Everything was changing dimension, changing in the air he breathed, as years before on October 16, 1938, it had changed in King Edward Street in his own small room.

Being so sensitive to change was like having an extra arm. You didn't know what to do with it or where to put it.

The signal Hogan expected to hear didn't sound.

There was no beating of the drum to announce the end of the world. He'd always seen himself jumping up to the sound and running like mad. The people he knew would come running towards him, all pale, all strained, all with faces like white-painted plaster, everything unearthly, everything silent, everything unbearable.

Each person would be running and running and

running, Heaven knew where. Running away from it or running to meet it, running, running.

But the drum didn't sound. Had it called him from the back of his mind and fallen silent before he awoke?

His heartbeat was leaping up until he could feel it leaping in his temples, and he was reaching for his glasses with care.

'Don't drop them, Hogan,' he said.

From the look of his watch it was about five-thirty.

He squirmed into his shorts and shirt and broke out through the mosquito net and touched with bare feet for the palm-mat floor.

It was so dark. It wasn't fair.

It was good to find the floor. It was a relief of magnitude that his sandals were exactly there, his feet sliding into them without difficulty or pause. He buckled them quickly, securely.

His heartbeat was taking his breath away. He was panting as if he had run too hard too far.

He groped along the wall for the door, scared, with a pain in his stomach and electricity shocking his nerves.

Outside the night was alive.

The huts back there were unlit, though he could never be sure. The huts were half-a-mile. No faint slit of lamp-light glimmered anywhere among the palms. Perhaps children were not awake for a change and the Brigadier was not pacing the night through, as he'd been known to do when his calm was disturbed.

Nothing moved. No one called.

The night was shapeless back there. Armies of Japanese could have crept through the hut lanes and no one would have known they were there. They could have slit a throat each and quietly gone.

'They're unusual,' people were saying, 'they're unnatural,' though people had no experience to prove the point. 'The Japanese don't make noise.'

Makes sense to me, Hogan said; if it's war, why muck around?

It was alive out there, like spiders running wild.

He passed round the hut to the weather-side and screwed his eyes into the night, to where the cliff bulked huge. There must have been high cloud unless every star in the Universe had died, yet the cliff was visible there, though not a trace of day or dawn showed.

Hogan's legs began to feel heavy and dull and disabled, as in a dream, as if lifting them to make the next step would be beyond his strength or nerve.

The electricity was in the air like a storm.

'You up on that cliff, Jon Griffiths. Shouldn't you be beating the drum? Shouldn't everybody be rushing out of the huts and running like mad?'

He spoke only to himself, and his speech thickened like congealing glue.

'Why am I alone out here?'

The sound he made was deep, strange, and stretched, as if stupefied by alcohol.

Why did Jon Griffiths on the cliff appear not to care?

Why was Hogan Hancock down here collapsing with nerves?

'God gave you your instincts to use,' the Brigadier said during an inspection of the guard. 'Don't ignore them. I'm relying on you, Hogan, all the clock round. Sensitivity's your strength. We're endeavouring to invoke powers outside our understanding. If you think something's happening, act, act, act.'

There were things for Hogan Hancock and things for Jon Griffiths both to do.

'If you fail,' the Brigadier said. . . 'Well, I can't see that far. Failure or success: who can tell what either might be or what either might bring?'

Procedures were laid down, like fire drill in an explosives factory or lifeboat drill at sea. Hogan should have acted out the motions instinctively, but his instinct for action had gone.

All Hogan could find were instincts for feeling and fearing and wanting to hide. The best way to hide was never to be born.

In his memory he saw the crowd rise up among the

seats and the aisles of the Bijou on September 22, 1940, a thought like a red traffic signal flashing in his mind.

'*Brigadier! Brigadier!*'

A thousand souls rising as one, with one shout; a thousand return-sprung seats springing back like a fusillade of guns.

There stood the Brigadier at the edge of the stage, transported, transformed.

'*Brigadier! Brigadier!*'

In Europe they were rising in the great halls and on the parade grounds. 'Heil Hitler! Heil Hitler!'

There were people who said the hysteria in the Bijou and the hysteria in Europe made the same sound.

'Hogan Hancock, MOVE.'

Hogan heard the command, as mighty as the call that made the Bijou stand.

No one was around, but he moved.

The cliff glowed.

Hogan ran as he had known he would.

He ran with his face like white-painted plaster, and everything was unearthly and silent and unbearable, as he had known it would be.

This could be the end of the world and he was only sixteen.

Twenty-One

(September 22, 1940)

One should try to come to the principal events of Operation Sword in an orderly manner. All actions should be seen to follow others. Each effect should have its cause, provided one calls the originating cause the mystery and ignores it.

But this shows up the error of trying to place any happening in an orderly sequence. The farther back one stretches towards any starting point, the more obscured the starting point is seen to be, and the more we are forced to admit that nothing has a beginning we can accurately define. So the more we must wonder whether all life is locked into a cycle that goes eternally round.

The conflict arises between the need to tell the truth and the hope of being believed, whilst meeting the obligation of recording all matters known – even those apparently of no importance – relating to Operation Sword, or Scabbard, or the God Squad, or the T. T. Mission, or 'For Pity's Sake, Mr Prime Minister, Shut the Brigadier Up and Let Him Go, He's Driving Us Mad,' as the establishment on Tangu Tangu variously became known, according to the particular departmental dustbin into which the records afterwards were thrown.

How was it that these events ever came to happen? Why were they allowed to happen? Did governments – or gods – care so little? Not much relating to those terrible years suggests that human life had value beyond that given to something you threw away.

Twenty-Two

(September 22, 1940)

That Sunday, as usual, Kerry's father was in the workshop behind his house in Prince Consort Place.

He propelled a stool towards his daughter and said, 'Sit down.' Then went on shaping the cow-catcher for a model of an early locomotive of the Atchison, Topeka and Santa Fe. In his view the name of the railroad was one of the delights of language.

In the background a radio was turned low. He was waiting for news of the Battle of Britain.

'I can't sit down, Father,' Kerry said. 'There isn't time.'

She had only a moment to peck his cheek, or her mother would be tooting in the road.

'What nonsense.' His voice was unnaturally loud. 'Try bending at the knees. It's done in a jiffy.'

She thought he was joking, though she thought it was strange. 'Mother's ready to leave for the Bijou.'

'If I can spend Sundays on my own for four years, your mother can wait for a minute on the road.'

An astonishment bounced inside Kerry.

'How often do we see each other?' he said.

Her breath caught. 'Often, Father. All the time.'

'Yes. Across a room or passing by. A hand held out for money. A bill somewhere to pay. I asked you to sit.'

She was shaken, and the horn of the Wolseley sounded from the road.

'Mother's going to be cross,' she said lamely, but sat on the stool.

'I see good things getting away. Remember them? They changed when your mother joined the bigots. I never thought you'd join, too.'

Kerry was breathless, and felt bloodless. Her father valued peace about the house. Even above his rights, and sometimes above his dignity.

'I want you,' he said loudly, 'to temper your enthusiasms for your brigadier. I want you to *think*. I want you to be *concerned* for the people this odd God of his rejects.'

She became cold.

'You're special, Kerry,' he said, 'a special human being. One of God's children. I used to say, how can it be you came of me? I can't allow scars like this to appear without protest.'

The cold reached to her hands.

'I beg of you,' he said, 'to feel compassion for fellow Europeans who come from outside your brigadier's narrow focus. I beg of you to feel more than patronage for fellow human beings whose noses or skins differ from your own.'

She started shivering.

'I am dismayed by what I hear at my own dining-table. Human beings like yourself put by your brigadier outside God's scheme for the world, outside His love and pity. The arrogance of your brigadier, or the arrogance of his little god. What god is he talking about? I thought we left tribal ideas behind centuries ago. Whose blood runs pure like a mountain stream these days, with thousands of years of lovers gone before us? Do I hear echoes of Nazidom in my own house? What is *pure*, I'd like to know. Not your blood, young lady.'

He was pale and passionate.

'What of the Germans, the millions scared stiff like you and me? Ordinary fathers and daughters, like you and me. Ordinary mothers and sons. Afraid for each other every hour, but unable to do anything about it except *toe the line*; their thinking processes poisoned by pernicious propaganda. In a society like theirs it's death to take an opposing stand. In a society like ours it's hard enough and we're free to do as we please. What do you know of the S.S. or the Gestapo? Would you care to stand up in the streets of Berlin and shout Hitler down? When your brigadier won his medals he had a gun in his hand.'

To herself, Kerry said, 'This man is a fool.'

'What do we know of rifle butts crashing through doors in the middle of the night? What does your brigadier know of it or of anything else that the act portends or implies? I tell you, if anyone survives the next few years, we'll owe it to our young men. We'll owe it to their broken bodies and their broken lives. We'll not be owing it to ideas like these of your latter-day brigadier. He might have been a hero once, my girl. Not now. You may go.'

Kerry went, white, sick, violent, with tears of rage bright in her eyes.

'I hate him,' she said aloud. She said it to the cracks in the garden path, to the rose bushes, and the wistaria, and the velvet-surfaced lawn, and the crabapples in bloom.

'I hate him. How could he do this to me? How could he say things like it about my lovely man?'

Her mother was waiting on the road in the Wolseley, impatiently sounding the horn.

Twenty-Three

(English Summer of 1923 — September 22, 1940)

On Sunday 22 September, 1940, the doors of the Bijou Theatre were opened at midday, Mr Padraig O'Riordan making his way with the keys through the props being set down on the pavement from Chisholm's furniture van.

'Every Sunday this mess on me footpath,' complained O'Riordan, who came down from his residence on The Hill to turn the key. 'It's a valuable property, this picture theatre. I got real velvet on the seats and me chandeliers come from Venice. There's no replacin' them with a war on. I got the best Yankee projection equipment and there's no replacin' that neither. I got English carpet and when will you get anythin' out of England again? I got statues what are genuine copies from Greece and Rome and nothin's come out of there in a thousand years. I'm runnin' no risks of youse religious fanatics leavin' me doors ajar. Never got nothin' I didn't work me fingers to the bone for. Gimme me rent and I'll be back at five to lock up.'

'It's a Jerry-built monstrosity,' was the opinion of Mrs Shuffle. 'I wish we could find a less frivolous meeting hall. The Brigadier should be heard in the great houses of assembly. This lack of what is right for serious occasions is a deprivation of life in the colonies.'

Mrs Shuffle had a grand way with words, as with most things, though Kerry was her finest achievement. Even classmates at Kerry's expensive college for young ladies, themselves cursed with pimples and figures like footballers, looked upon her with respect. And gentlemen, of most ages, agreed that the wonders of human generation were wonders indeed. How could this exquisite creature be the daughter of Victoria Alexandra Shuffle?

Mrs Shuffle based her informed opinion of the Bijou upon her overseas experience, having lived in England for the summer of 1923. Her admiration for the English embraced the way they made their cloth, the way they built their palaces, the way they cooked their beef, the way they modulated their vowel sounds, the way they crowned their kings, even the way they walked to the train with bowler hats on.

'The English are the salt of the Earth by which the human race has been salted,' she wrote during September, 1940. 'Upon English institutions and literature, upon English religious piety and political innovation, the ultimate ascent of the human race out of darkness must be seen to stand. It is our national privilege as men and women of British origin to stand beside them.'

Mrs Shuffle rounded the words in front of the mirror (they were known as *Thought of the Week*), and rounded them further in the privacy of her bath, and went on rounding them in public as she strode through the park, gesticulating. Then she typed four top copies on Committee notepaper, signed her name at the foot, and published them in the Society's advertisement in the daily newspapers of Saturday 21 September, 1940. Her telephone went on ringing until past 10 p.m. and when finally she retired for the night she was able to sleep with a smile on her face.

Mrs Shuffle liked to be regarded as an Anglophile, though some with a streak of malice called her a cliché. Kerry, having first heard rumours of this when she was eight, searched for *cleeshay* in the Oxford English Dictionary. Cliché, it said, the French name for a stereotype block.

It became stranger when she looked up *stereotype*.

Mrs Shuffle was sometimes considered to be a widow woman, though no one remembered the funeral and no one had sent flowers. Mr Shuffle was a quiet fellow who bought and sold stocks and shares and built locomotives out of matchsticks.

Shufflebottom was the family name, fully spelt out, and pronounced Shawf'll-boe-thum by Mrs Shuffle, when pressed, as at Polling Booths on Voting Days, but differently by Mr Shuffle who said, 'What the hell.'

'The Bijou,' Mrs Shuffle said in committee, 'looks like a mad wedding cake.'

People like the Hancocks thought the Bijou gave the district a touch of class.

The Brigadier said, 'Public buildings disturb people, Mrs Shuffle. In the Bijou they are relaxed, eager for a story, anxious to become involved.'

Usually you sat there in the dark, anyway, to watch a film, and Mrs Shuffle's feelings didn't matter, but on Sunday afternoons under the bright lights her feelings were decisive. She was, after all, Executive Secretary of the Society for World Order under Divine Rule (1936), and even if the Brigadier made light of Paddy O'Riordan's taste, Mrs Shuffle would not tolerate it while she had the option to obscure it.

The transformation began with the sandwich board erected on the pavement as it came down from Chisholm's van.

S.W.O.R.D.
PATRIOTIC RALLY HERE TODAY
2.45
Community Singing, Soloists
Camberwell City Brass Band

BRIGADIER HON. MATTHEW PALMER
D.S.O., M.C., M.L.A.
Walk in
It's free

'Here we are then,' Mrs Shuffle said, sweeping into the foyer with an armful of early roses, followed by lesser members of the committee and jostling youngsters. 'Turn *that* affront to the wall! The Oomph Girl, they call her. Pigs and potato sacks! With respect, we'll have King George hung there, the Queen there, the Princesses in the alcove, and the Royal Coat of Arms above the door. We'll have the book table on this side today with prominence, please, Mrs MacWhorter, to *Dunkirk Explained*, and the tea table on that side, with the urn switched *on*, Mrs Griffiths, *if* you don't mind! Are you ready with the extension ladder, Mr Chambers? Take it on through.'

Mr Chambers had been ready with the extension ladder and taking it on through for four and a half years.

'Now you boys who work with Mr Chambers; this week I'll have the statuary decently attired, all blatant areas covered by Union Jacks, and I will not tolerate their falling away. I will never believe that Boy Scouts with merit badges genuinely encounter the slightest difficulty with such elementary knots.'

The statuary consisted of seven Satyrs, together with Diana, Hermes, Apollo, and Venus. Last King's Birthday Sunday, in the course of the Oath of Allegiance to the Crown, Diana and Venus and one Satyr with a smile painted on its face disrobed simultaneously, Union Jacks fluttering over the auditorium like veils.

'Stun me,' the Brigadier had murmured, standing to attention.

'A nice touch of pageantry,' was the comment of the Reverend Pearce home on indefinite leave from Tangu Tangu, 'though what do you do with a flag ten feet long when it falls on your head during prayers?'

Mrs Shuffle said, 'I'll kill the little perishers.'

A magnificent sight the Bijou was, just the same, reminiscent of the famous chapel at Windsor, which was Mrs Shuffle's intention.

Your heart lifted as you walked in. Banners and flags hung long all around. Flags of the Empire; all those far-off colonies with exotic names. The flag of the United States of America. Flags of the Scandinavians and the heraldic emblems of minorities vanished behind the new frontiers of Europe. But not the flag of the French Republic.

'Over my body, dead and buried,' said the Brigadier.
He didn't care for the French.
He never said why.

Twenty-Four

(September 22, 1940)

Hundreds who walked through the door of the Bijou that day knew the history of the world could change before they had time to walk out. It was a world-wide tension touching all people, a world-wide coming to the brink. While *God Save the King* was sung, while the prayers were read, the walls of the pit at the feet of the British race were breaking. In the pit lay the unimaginable, said to be the greatest evil of a thousand years.

Each tap of Hogan's finger might be it. The end of the British Empire. The beginning of the death.

Hogan tapped the middle finger of his right hand into the hollow under his right knee. When he stood for the Oath of Allegiance he tapped the finger into his hip. When he stood for the Star-Spangled Banner he tapped the under-surface of the hymn sheet, causing it to flutter.

'Stop it,' his father hissed.

Hogan slipped his fingers under his lapel and tapped his collar-bone.

Jon Griffiths stood round eyed, feeling helpless, realizing, awkwardly, that he was in fear for his life, though he didn't yet carry a gun or live within a month's journey of the front line.

Kerry stood white and tense and hurt by hate. Living in the glow of the Brigadier was a world removed from her father's mindless accusations. To be numbered among the chosen was not to secure a life of privilege. It was to live a life of service to the human race, the whole race, to uplift it, to refine it in spirit and in truth. She'd march with her Brigadier, the Cross of St George upon her breast-plate, God's light in her eyes.

The MacWhorter twins sang in harmony and held each other by the hand. If the Nazis came and killed Jessie, what would Phoebe do? If they killed Phoebe, what would Jessie do? She'd put her head in the gas oven, if there was any gas. Or her finger in the light socket, if there was any electricity. Or she'd rush to a high place and leap off.

How many were left of the young men in Royal Air Force blue? Those not dead yet, or gone missing yet, in the few overstressed aircraft not shot full of holes yet, or worn-out yet? If they fell in combat, or fell from fatigue, or fell from the magnitude of what they were being asked each day to do, the world fell with them.

Then, mile by mile, and year by year, every Jew in every land and every independent mind would hang or burn. Until they came to you. You'd be strung up somewhere, or put against the wall and gunned down, or chained into a labour gang to perish by deprivation, or your body outraged and thrown out with the garbage. You prayed it might be an exaggeration. You hoped it was the ultimate lie against your fellow man.

Foolish prayer. Foolish hope. Everything was true, you knew.

The great contralto, late of Covent Garden – late of La Scala also, before the Italians started goosestepping – came to the edge of the Bijou stage, as if to the edge of the pit. A trumpeter came with her, but stood apart.

A stillness was there, for her son had died in a Spitfire but eight days gone. She had nothing now except her fame.

The trumpeter played the opening bars of a famous song:

Land of Hope and Glory, Mother of the Free,
How shall we extol thee, who are born of thee?
Wider still and wider shall thy bounds be set;
God who made thee mighty, make thee mightier yet.*

*A. C. Benson, 1862–1925.

Hundreds saw the great contralto draw breath, but she bowed her head and made no sound. The trumpeter held back his note and the hush came down.

Remote from herself she heard stirrings like strong winds and sounds like machine-guns and saw her son coming to her through clouds. He was twenty-one.

Perhaps around her, or within a nave inside her head, a thousand voices sang. There were trombones and horns and drums and a trumpeter. The words were familiar.

A giant at her side closed a hand on her arm.

'Madam.'

The thousand voices were there, out there, coming from the blur. A thousand faces took shape, singing her song.

'You're not alone, Madam, as you can see. We need to sing it for you. Allow us, please.'

It began to happen then. Hogan felt it happening and started shivering. Jon, in a few moments, was shaking uncontrollably and could barely sing the words. Kerry felt the passing of hatred and the coming of warmth, height, distance and magnitude. Jessie and Phoebe held hands, held on, fingers interlocking until they hurt. The thousand people there felt as one. It wasn't just the Brigadier. Or the great contralto and the spirit of her son. Or Cunningham and Hawkins and Mrs Victoria Alexandra Shuffle rising to their feet as if one nerve prompted them. For the thousand rose up with them and the fusillade of seats was the fusillade of guns, and the trumpet and the trombones and the drums. And Britain at the brink. And the Royal Air Force, the world upon its shoulders, the world carried by boys. And the great imperial song, the song of the rulers, sung by the subjects, with love. Together, knowingly and unknowingly, they made it happen.

Centre-stage, the Brigadier and the great contralto leant against each other, or seemed to, until the song was almost sung and the applause had begun. Intensity of feeling blurred the details. Everything seemed to happen at the one time, but could not have done. Details had to occur in order, but who could separate them? Not Hogan.

Not Jon.

The song and the applause and the emotion and the Brigadier's huge performance were part of a single experience that happened like the Angel of Mons.

If you were there, you could never deny it. It was huge beyond belief, but it happened. It happened and you were in it.

'I was there and it happened,' said Jon, stunned.

One thousand persons went home afterwards, stunned. 'I was there,' each said, 'and it happened.'

The Brigadier made his way back to his apartment in the Windsor Hotel across the street from State Parliament House. He locked the outer door. He poured a long hard whisky. He sat at his desk, knuckles white, body rigid.

'I was there,' he said, 'and it happened. God speaking through me? It can't be. What have I done?'

The telephone started ringing.

The great contralto had not sung a syllable of her song, but the applause began and went on and on. It was for her, and for the Royal Air Force, and for her son. For Winston Churchill and Dunkirk as well. Was it symbolic of the hardening will of people who had felt themselves to be lost? Was it the firing in the blood of fighter aircraft engines? Or the marching of feet and a rising shout? Was it the Brigadier's spirit becoming a visible light?

They became as one person with him, hearing and speaking his words inside themselves, living his words, as if knowing each word before he uttered it, believing his words, believing in him.

A great presence moved among them and told them what to do. Told him, too.

Late that night in his apartment, after the telephone finally fell silent, the Brigadier first wrote in his Doomsday Book. It was a green leather-bound journal of three hundred foolscap leaves, given him by his Campaign Committee after the State Elections in 1932, and never before used.

Twenty-Five

The declaration of Matthew Palmer, bachelor, first recorded at Melbourne, Australia, on September 22, 1940:

I, Matthew Palmer, soldier, member of parliament, declare that until this day I have regarded myself with some amusement. Now I cannot say if I am prophet, rogue, or fool, for if I am a prophet God has touched me and who am I that God should single me out? Yet if God has not touched me, I am a rogue, that such predictions and promises should come from my lips before a thousand and seventy witnesses.

This day, I have committed myself to a course of action that can only end in unimaginable terror or my own disgrace.

I was born in Bendigo, Australia, on January 25, 1892. My Father, Leonard Melville Palmer, was the fourth son of Sir Thomas Palmer, Bart, of Guildford, England. My mother, Hilary Jane, was the second daughter of Robert Willoughby of Willoughby River Downs in the State of New South Wales. I was the sole issue. My mother died at my birth.

I was educated at Willoughby River Downs and the University of Sydney. I enlisted in the army on August 8, 1914, was commissioned on October 1, 1914, and subsequently served in Egypt, Gallipoli, Palestine, and on the Western Front. I was awarded the Distinguished Service Order, the Military Cross, and was twice Mentioned in Dispatches. I was invalided home with multiple wounds in March, 1918, but continued as a soldier. I was Acting Chief of Staff during General Harrison's absence in 1928.

In May, 1932, I presented as a candidate for the Legislative Assembly in the State of Victoria and won my seat with a good majority. I have represented my electorate ever since, and have become much involved in issues of public concern, in the formal administration of hospitals, the patronage of charitable appeals, and the direction of major sporting bodies.

All are now seen to be minor issues beside S.W.O.R.D.

I am alleged to have founded S.W.O.R.D., as I am alleged to have founded several charities. I wear the charities with less discomfort. One's name becomes used or misused.

Was Victoria Shuffle the originating genius? I suspect so. Or possibly Jeffrey Hawkins. In May, 1936, we three were talking over dinner in the dining-room of this hotel, a political matter. I am politically obligated to both. I drank too much. The conversation changed. I had heard it before, notably that the Anglo-Saxon-Celtic populations of Britain and the U.S.A. were composed of elements of the lost tribes of Israel and could claim to be God's agents in the world. This might be said to be cosy – if you're British or American.

It is thus untrue to suggest that I originated the theme of S.W.O.R.D., though I invented the name. The idea has been around for generations, at least. Generally speaking, I see it as a harmless but absorbing study, and who can say with conviction it is right or wrong? I've spent numerous hours in recent years studying scriptures and documents, both ancient and modern, and am no more certain now – for the case or against it – than I was at the outset.

The components of the theory come together like the solution to a puzzle, but to my mind there always seems to be a missing piece, where one must resort to a bridging act of faith. Scholarship of this kind is not sound.

If I am guilty, my guilt lies here, in allowing my person and name to be used, whilst not being sure of my ground. Yet I am told I said to Victoria and Jeffrey, 'Jolly good. Go ahead. Go ahead.' So having given my word, I found myself committed to a public stance on the matter.

Today the crown, if crown it be, becomes my crown of thorns. Today I have given my word again before many witnesses that I will re-establish a direct physical link between God and Earth, in the ancient Biblical tradition.

I said these things. I heard myself as if listening to another person. I saw the people rise up, calling my name. It was as if my body were afire.

It is an insult to God, I said, that the fate of this world should

116

reside in Adolf Hitler. Who is Hitler that he should own God's world and people? We know God intervenes in world events when implored by His people. We are His people. When the King calls the Empire to prayer, Dunkirk happens. This is a miracle in our own day and age. God thus points the way and proves His promises. His promises though ancient are not ancient beyond recall. They continue until here and now.

God will confront Adolf Hitler with fire. If we ask Him, God will come with his Heroes to light up the world again, to drive out the darkness.

An evil beyond human calculation is destroying us. None but a Good beyond human calculation can crush the evil.

God has given us freedom of will and can come into the world only if we invite him in sincerity and belief.

S.W.O.R.D. thus declares itself to be man's agent against the great evil.

S.W.O.R.D. will establish the frontier, the observation post. Out in front, S.W.O.R.D. will establish the forward post from which the prayers go up and back through which God may enter.

God's finger has touched us.

We will establish the ultimate weapon against Hitler. We will establish the mission to save the world. We will not talk about it. We will do it. I promise. Follow me.

Amazed, I heard myself. For in the past I had used S.W.O.R.D. as S.W.O.R.D. had used me. I had used it to expound my own ideas and my own politics – and why not? It bore my name. I had the right to express myself if I accepted the responsibility. But when our great contralto wept, S.W.O.R.D. was used – as I was used – by something from the outside. A power touched me. I knew that God would come into the world to save the world and that He would stay to fulfil the promise of a thousand perfect years – if S.W.O.R.D. prepared the way. At once. Now.

These predictions and promises came from my mouth. The power that used me knows I am honourable. The power knows I have accepted favours properly given, but have never been bought. The power knows I have never been corrupted.

I pray God is the power.

I know not where this will lead us, but I will make it happen.

I have promised.

Twenty-Six

(February 12, 1942)

The lamp on the Brigadier's table burnt low, sputtering. It threw a quality of shadow rather than a quality of light; a murky pool barely large enough to sight the page and direct the pen.

The smell of the smoke, the soot of the flame, soiled the humid air of the hut and brought a hard clot of phlegm to his throat and turned black the stains of his sweat.

Impurities were in the lighting kerosene, rain-water at the least. There was little that rain had not damaged.

Moths fluttered against the lamp glass. Poor witless creatures. And fell into the chimney on to the flame. Every morning the sooted glass had to be cleaned. Every night the open Doomsday Book crawled with insects until he brushed them aside, smearing their substance on page after page. Night after night, with a rubber, he erased the fabric of the creatures, the smears, and obscured them by writing over of human events and deeds.

Were the lives of humans as unimportant to the gods?

Was it that someone else in another place wrote of the deeds of the gods in a greater book and smeared the fabric of humans like moths across the page?

The Brigadier thought about it.

February 12. Thursday. My foreboding becomes a pain that never gives me peace, that never lets me sleep. When did I last sleep at peace? Rarely since the event in the Bijou on September 22, 1940.

How near are the Japanese?

What terrible thing have I done, bringing women and children into this defenceless place?

Do we oppose their aeroplanes with stones?

Do we fight their battleships with sticks?

Especially, I fear for the youngsters, trusting in me as prophet and soldier, not knowing of the wounds upon my spirit, not aware of my limitations, not understanding that ten thousand men might not hold this place against such an enemy.

The youngsters turn my way as if to put the question. I see it in their eyes. I have seen it in Kerry's eyes also. The heart moves me to comfort her, but I cannot.

How unresponsive the ocean lies. Never yielding up sound or sight of a friend. Every way I look, for as far as I look, the ocean lies unresponsive, not caring.

God sends no visions or realities.

No one has tried to reach us, I am certain. They rid themselves of us, and were glad to be rid of the embarrassment of my petitions and proclamations, which compounds the blame I must bear.

Or are they not able to reach us? Is our defeat so great? Are we to hope the Americans may recover from Pearl Harbor and pass this way? But when? Which year?

Am I to venture with the people on to the sea without properly constructed boats? In the cyclone season? Do we commit women and children to rafts? Who knows where the currents flow or the winds blow?

On this island each of us is living out the end. Here each of us will die. Day by day more come to suspect it. The spirit of our prayers weakens, although the fearful fervour increases.

I am sick from the weariness of waiting. From the solitude of it. For if I prepare to oppose the Japanese beyond steps already taken, I openly declare our failure. If I make my lines of retreat clearer to see, all will observe that their lives are about to be lost for nothing, that their mission has been my vanity, and that their destruction will be the outcome.

Oh, for effective lines of communication between our key points. That I failed to bring army signals equipment was the blindness of a foolish faith or a criminal self-deceit.

These Japanese wage war in merciless dimensions.

I have no communications, no weapons to speak of, and an unhelpful terrain. For me to oppose these Japanese is absurd.

They ride so high, so wide, so handsome. What remains to oppose them but distance?

Will they come tomorrow? Will I live until they come? For want of sleep I am exhausted beyond imagination. I put down my head but turn ceaselessly. Every bone and joint aches, aches. My brain wishes for stillness, for silence. Is it not a miracle that the human frame can bear it?

Each night and in the morning, there I am with the question that has overwhelmed the prophets. Why had God gone silent? Why should He touch me, then go away?

Each day my prayers are lost in an empty place. They pass out along empty corridors into empty rooms. I am almost mad for want of sleep, but He hears me not.

Has He saved even His world of elements and growing things from the greed and ignorance of men? Has He spared the dumb animals? Has He healed the deserts? Has He held back the catastrophes of Nature? Or is the condition made worse for living creatures because He doesn't care, because He uses catastropnes to create new shapes for His amusement?

Has He lost sight of us? Has He gone on making more and more worlds in a fever of Creation, reaching out farther and farther and deeper and deeper and leaving each, in turn, to rot?

Is He a million years away now? To which new worlds does He send His messengers?

Have our prayers become the bleatings of sheep?

What sheep by bleating in the stockyards was not cut up for meat?

Forgive me, but You have gone from me left me sleepness and taken from me my will to live.

Twenty-Seven

(February 16, 1942)

5.30 a.m., plus or minus one minute.
oo degrees 30 minutes South, 146 degrees 50 minutes
East.

Hogan's state of mind changed as he sprinted for the
rising face of the cliff, as he left the sentry hut behind, as he
sprinted into the darkness, into the presence of the glow.
Awake; wider awake than he had ever been; drawing from
deep wells of energy. His face and body changed, though
he was not aware of it. He changed into something less
than human and something considerably more.

Hogan transported himself from the sentry hut to the
look-out hundreds of yards distant in an interval he would
have ridiculed or feared to consider in the light of day.

He drew huge breaths that powered him, that
sharpened his sight and steadied his stride, that lent him a
sureness and fleetness and breadth of vision he had not
known before.

He didn't lose the winding path, didn't run short of
wind, didn't stumble or fall. Desperation and exhilaration
were parts of it, at exceptional levels. A super-charge of
adrenalin propelled him like a stone skipping over a pond.

A long electric moment waited at the clifftop, into
which he came with surprise, where he was permitted to
glimpse a stupendous happening somewhere between its
coming and its going.

Hogan was given a special view of a whole wide world,
off frequency from the real world. Components of what he

saw did not return to mind until minutes later and they returned then at the flood. Areas of darkness and light with dire meanings lay around him. In the midst Jon was asleep, a step or two from the booth, his head fallen between his knees. A touch might turn him into a ball, might roll him off the cliff to bounce in the sea far beneath. Beyond Jon, far away, an area of eastern sky low to the horizon looked like an exploding star.

Hogan thought, 'The Heroes of Light.'

He said, 'Jon, why are you asleep?'

There was no voice. In Hogan's head the question was clear, but in reality the words emerged like air, and no one, waking or sleeping, could have heard them other than Hogan.

He dropped a hand to Jon's shoulder and Jon leapt up with a cry. 'Oh no. Oh no.'

Jon's senses swam from the shock, but Hogan was there, not the Brigadier, Hogan with an arm raised gesturing into the east.

The relief made Jon feel ill.

What was Hogan doing out of bed? He never appeared before 6 a.m. Hogan looking alarmingly strange, as if his bones had turned to stone. His arm remained raised, making an accusation. So Jon squinted into the east, consciously confused, but below that level doing sums that sprang to prominence.

How often had he estimated the number of stars in a given area of sky? 'Two hundred stars!' How often had he followed the estimation with a precise count of 190, say, or 210, or closer?

The feeling of nausea began to spread. He began to shake along with it.

'Grief. There'd be a hundred separate lights.'

His breath was catching. Bearing the degree of fright wasn't easy.

He searched with the binoculars then, as rehearsed a thousand times since the sighting of the ship two hundred and five night-watches ago.

'Different from stars,' he said breathlessly. 'They could

be a hundred miles away. How do you judge distance when you don't know what they are? Couldn't be aeroplanes. You couldn't see aeroplanes that far away.'

Hogan's voice might have come out of a tunnel. 'You know what they've got to be. You know. You know.'

Jon shut his eyes tightly against the lenses. Opened them. The lights were still there.

'Are they fires? Real fires?'

His mind poured over with all the doubts he had ever felt. In they poured and out they swept, leaving the fears, leaving the fires. Was the world about to burn?

Hogan was sinking to his knees, as if the stone in his bones had gone to soft clay.

'Hogan!'

Hogan continued to subside and Jon made a grab for him, but glimpsed the drum, the cylinder, long ago struck on Tangu Tangu to warn the islanders of the European sailing ship offshore. There it hung from the crossbar beside the booth. Now silent. Warning no one.

Jon leapt for the mallet, swung for the drum, and mallet and drum met through his hands, arms and shoulders, the impact striking to his heart. It was an appalling consequence, the sound and the shock of what it meant, of what the signal conveyed, yet the pitch was as mellow as gamelan on a Javenese breeze.

Each strike of the mallet, each spasm of the rhythm, built the fright blow upon blow and level upon level.

He thought of holes in the ground and wished he were half-a-mile down.

'It's happening,' he said, striking the drum.

Those poor people. All the poor people in the huts below. In the confusion of night and fright. His parents. His young brother. All those poor people shocked out of sleep, stumbling over each other, against the booming of the signal drum, booming like heartbeats, warning them of no one knew what.

Kerry was down there.

'It's the end of us, Kerry,' he said, striking the drum, 'and we never even started.'

In the sky he could see the end coming like a dawn.
Fire. Real fire.

It was happening.

Jon went on striking the drum, blow upon blow upon blow, until his head could have split and every muscle in his body hurt, as if striking it a hundred times more would make up for having struck it late.

Twenty-Eight

(February 16, 1942)

Inside her head Kerry heard a beat similar to the heartbeat that plagued her at bed-time. Then, no matter which way she put her head, it relayed through her temples and seemed always about to stop. If it stopped she'd never remake the world with her Brigadier.

'Kerry, wake up.'

Her mother's voice intruded with unaccustomed harshness, urgently, as somewhere an object fell. There were stumbling sounds in the darkness.

Kerry jerked up into a tangle of mosquito net that dropped about her like an animal trap. She waved her arms to ward it off.

The heartbeat was not in her head. It was in the bunk. In the air. Everywhere.

The heartbeat was the Tangu Tangu signal drum and her own heartbeat leapt up on an edge.

Voices were in the air also, outside.

A hammering shook the wall.

'*Mrs Shuffle. Do you hear?*'

'Yes, yes.'

In a moment the hammering moved to the hut next door.

'*Don McBride. Do you hear?*'

The camp guards were crashing along each lane.

Someone rang the school-bell.

'Out of bed, Kerry. Hurry. The Japanese.'

That old-time ladder of sword-blades reared in front of Kerry.

In the dark, how was she to climb the ladder? Did she meet the Japanese half-way? No way up then, and no way down. Kerry in the middle, stranded, trapped, killed.

She clawed the net aside. 'My clothes!'

'Wear anything you can find.'

The drum was still beating. The bell was still ringing. Both made everything worse. She wished they'd stop. How could you think above it?

A match struck and the flame quickly crossed the hut to the candle. In the flame, in the flare, Kerry blinked into her mother's frightened face, her bun unwound, her hair long and disordered and fluffy and soft. Few had seen Victoria Shuffle looking less like herself.

Something struck Kerry. Almost every tooth in her head showed. 'Mother! That's not the signal for the Japanese!'

Victoria Shuffle's face changed. Extraordinary. Extraordinary. As if the substance of her flesh changed. Her lips moved, 'Eruption? Earthquake?' But she shook her head to see her own silent words. The match scorched her fingers and dropped to the floor.

'Kerry. It's not the signal for the Japanese. . . Quickly. Quickly. Dress quickly.'

'The Brigadier's right,' Kerry said.

'I was right,' Victoria Shuffle said.

Kerry felt a sudden magnanimity towards her father who had not believed. She forgave him, and said, 'Mother, it's the signal for God's coming. Are we to see God?'

'Hurry, dear.'

Outside a woman's voice turned piercing, as if to bridge a mile. '*For Pity's sake, Jon, that can't be the signal you mean.*'

Was it Jon's mother?

'Hallelujah,' called the Everards, as if orchestrated. They called it again and again across the din and the shouting.

A woman or child became hysterical. The sound was unreal, like unhinged laughter. Several children were crying. Christopher McBride began wailing.

Was this uproar what the Brigadier had hoped for S.W.O.R.D.?

The voice of Jeff Hawkins came strongly over the top through a megaphone. 'Attention. Attention. The signal warns of Contingency A. You must be calm.'

Kerry plunged into some kind of clothing.

'God's coming.'

She could grasp the idea, but couldn't. Part of her rushed forth to meet it, rejoicing, but there was a prodigious question, like a guilt.

Victoria Shuffle said, 'Am I to meet the Lord with my hair down? Kerry, that dress will not do unless you pin the neck.'

Cunningham strode through the hut lanes, his voice amplified. 'The head of each household will account for all members. Come to the beach empty-handed. Move with purpose. Be calm. Be calm.'

A man's cry cut across Cunningham. 'My boy's out there on his own. What about my boy? Does he have to face it alone?'

It had to be Hancock or Griffiths.

'Shoes on, Kerry? Did you pin the neck?'

Hawkins called, 'Make haste to the beach.'

Kerry broke out through the hut door.

Candlelight flickered on every side. Every opening hut spilled out its measure of people, its measure of noise, its measure of light.

The drum beat and the spasms of the school bell *pushed* her. They should have stopped the noise. It was confusing and destructive.

Victoria Shuffle called, 'Wait for me.'

Kerry heard only in part.

'Kerry, wait.'

Kerry ran on, ran away, side-stepping others as if repelled by auras of opposing energy. They belonged to a life now over, now gone. Would they meet again in some unimaginable place? Then the thought left her. The real world went out of phase.

She ran to the Brigadier's hut, its door not flung wide as

most were, but ajar, as if it had failed to hold on the catch. She touched it compulsively, but shyly, believing she had a special right to be there. God would understand.

'Sir,' she said. 'Here I am.'

No light showed from the opening. No sound came from within.

'Sir, it's Kerry.'

The surrounding turmoil receded into a forgotten place. She was aware only of the silence beyond the door.

He had to be in there, she knew it, but her feeling was hesitant.

'*Sir. Are you all right? Answer me.*'

She edged the opening of the door wider. Blackness stood up in front of her, yet she knew where every solid object was placed; the table, the chairs, the radio, the lock-up cupboard, the bunk.

'Please, sir. Answer me.'

Nothing was there but stillness, touched with his presence.

She shuffled to the table, feeling her way lightly; an open book was there, a pen, an ink well, an oil lamp cold for hours, a bottle of exotic shape. A brandy bottle. The very shape her father used to buy.

Kerry began to cry.

She'd known he'd been bearing more than he could stand.

She stumbled to his bunk and the mosquito net was down and she found him senseless.

'Oh, sir.'

She pressed her head to his chest and felt the life there, felt the breathing.

Kerry went on crying, but shook at him until he stirred. He was unbelievably distant, unbelievably heavy. His voice was slurred. 'Go away. . . Sleep. . . Sleep. . .'

Kerry said, 'God mustn't find you like this, sir.'

She shut the door and shot the bolt, then groped back to the bunk and sat beside it on the floor.

Twenty-Nine

(February 16, 1942)

Hogan was drained beyond belief, as if the minute of his flight to the cliff-top had expended the life-force of a year and scored his body through with wounds of emptiness. But his mind filled with terrible images coming at the flood and Jon had to be told of them, for how could Jon have seen other than the lights.

The awesome lights of God.

'Jon, listen to me.'

The drumbeat didn't stop. Its impact and reverberations were like a chord that challenged imitation. 'Another day I'll look for it on the organ,' Hogan thought. A thought in isolation. 'Given that I live another day.'

'Jon, listen to me.'

Nothing outside Jon existed for Jon, except the awesome lights and the drum and the mallet that he swung in a frenzy, grunting at each blow, grating with each rapid breath, binoculars bouncing about his neck, striking hard at his chest.

He cried out, 'How long did I sleep? It's *never* happened before. Was it hours? Have they been coming from the stars for hours?'

'Listen to me,' Hogan said: Hogan on the ground beneath hearing or seeing.

Jon went on beating the drum.

'Stop that,' Hogan said. 'If they've not heard by now they're not going to hear at all. You should know about the aeroplanes that I saw in the dark. Many aeroplanes on an island or a ship. Some waiting in blocks like pieces on a chess board. Crewmen with goggles on in the cockpits. Lots of little windows like leadlights on top. Engines running. Propellers going round. Some climbing into the air. Others taking off. Beautiful shapes. More beautiful than our aeroplanes or any the Germans have. As beautiful as fish.'

But he said it in a moment, all of it in a moment, and it sounded like bubbles popping in a tank.

Hogan screamed in frustration, but the scream was trapped inside him.

He was full of knuckles and knots, full of aeroplanes and lights and matters closer yet, full of things he had to tell.

'JON.'

Hogan almost tore himself apart.

Out the word came, loud and clear, and he dragged himself up by a corner post until he clung as if strung to the crossbar of the booth, and strength started coming back.

'YOU'VE GOT TO LISTEN TO ME.'

The mallet slipped from Jon's hands and his arms fell long like an ape's, and limp.

'Aeroplanes,' Hogan shouted, waving at the dark sky in the north-west. 'Aeroplanes with red roundels. Japanese aeroplanes with bombs. Coming at us – or I'd never have seen them with my eyes shut, would I?'

Jon heard the thuddings of his own heart and the throbbings of his own head, and a new question. Is it a volcano hundreds of miles away? An unsettling question that he wished had come first, not last. Then he heard shouting.

'Ships as well as aeroplanes. Six coming from the north and four coming from the south. Altogether ten ships with guns coming at us. Japanese flags. Japanese ships. Hundreds of soldiers on the decks. Do you hear me? You must listen to me.'

Jon was incredulous. 'What aeroplanes? What ships? I told you they weren't aeroplanes. How can they be ships?' He dragged off his binoculars and pushed them at Hogan. 'What about an eruption? Couldn't it be that? We know there are islands like it in all directions.'

Hogan turned the glasses into the darkness far from the East.

'Not that way, you idiot,' shrilled Jon, more incredulous yet. 'You're blinder than a bat.'

'Ships, not hallucinations,' Hogan said.

Jon saw him pivot about a hundred degrees south.

'More ships,' Hogan said, with authority that took Jon aback. 'There they are! And I saw aeroplanes taking off – in my head! I don't know from where, but I do know for what. We're in trouble.' He offered the glasses back. 'Check for yourself! We've got ourselves a bundle, Griffiths. We've copped the lot.'

Jon was shocked by the fright, shocked by the doubt, shocked that he could have drummed the wrong signal to all the poor people stumbling in the dark.

He shrieked his anger at Hogan. 'You made me think they were God's lights!'

He brought the glasses so sharply to his eyes that he struck his nose a stinging blow.

They were tongues of fire. They were flames.

Were they the fires of God or the flames of Hell? Were they coming from Heaven or spewing from a volcano far away in the sea?

He shifted his search from the light to the dark west and felt himself falling into the pit. He cried out, 'God, I see ships. I do see ships.'

The infamy. He had slept on watch while Japanese ships approached.

Jon cried, 'I've done a terrible thing.'

Hogan had the mallet and launched the head of it into the drum. He counted a three-second pause and launched at the drum again. And went on counting out pauses and went on launching at the drum. In his mind were ships with hundreds of soldiers on deck; and aeroplanes with little windows like leadlights on top and bombs in their bellies underneath; and the awesome lights of God.

Thirty

(February 16, 1942)

Jessie and Phoebe dragged each other into the night, stumbled into the night, hand by hand, shocked awake into a scramble like tumbling in a barrel. You were all over the place. You collided. You got your clothes on only because they'd been laid out in order and the drill had been rehearsed. You stumbled into the night, terrified, because it was time to step over the line drawn across the end of the world. Through all your growing years, you'd grown with S.W.O.R.D., preparing to cross the line. Now you were afraid to go to it, almost afraid to breathe.

The idea was immense. Imagination could not confront it.

Their mother went off another way.

'Go, go,' they heard her cry, as she ran her other way – to Mr Tregellas, they had to suppose.

Jessie and Phoebe reached out to hold her back, pleading, though not aloud. 'Mum, you got us into this. Don't leave us on our own. Stay with us please.'

The whole wide world around them was throbbing as if bees in swarms were descending to the ground.

Their mother was gone from sight and hearing. Gone out of reach. Did they have a mother now?

Jessie bit her lip. 'She's been so good for so long. She loves him. We've got to understand.'

They had each other; they clutched each other; then ran along the middle lane past Richard Cunningham, half-dressed, shaking his head as if lost, with a megaphone in his hand. Past someone else hurrying with purpose in the wrong direction – someone who might have been Miss Martha Littlejohn or Sister Weatheral or Kerry Shuffle.

Out there in the lanes it was like the concourse of a railway station in a dream of frantic insecurity, all trains leaving at the same time, everyone rushing to different platforms, all departure whistles blowing, everyone locked into the pursuit of his own grim going. Unearthly. Unreal.

No. Unearthly it might have been, unreal it was not.

They heard a small boy's cry. 'I want to go back to bed, mummy.'

Inside Jessie cried, 'Me, too. Me, too.'

As they ran they tried to see out into the great darkness, but palms made a canopy to obscure the sky, and they tripped, and they stumbled, and needed all their sight for the ground.

'There's nothing looking like God up there,' Jessie said to herself, feeling tiny and terrified and alone, yet clutching all the while at Phoebe's hand. She'd not felt like it before, except when Phoebe had gone off on her own, forgetting to say where or why and taking hours to get back home.

'I thought He'd come like the sun,' Phoebe cried, 'all lit up. The sun's part of Him, isn't it? Isn't it?'

They lurched on through the coconut grove. It seemed to stretch for miles, but wasn't far. They got past the Everards who followed on each other's heels like a dog team, past probably the Olivers and the McCuskers, past probably the Hancocks, and others like shades sketched lightly at the sides.

They stumbled on to the narrow beach where the tide reduced the area of firm sand.

There spread the open sky, empty to the end of time. God, if coming in glory, was coming round another way.

The drum was beating, still beating.

Jessie and Phoebe clutched tighter with shaking, clammy hands, barely able to think, barely able to stand. They held each other up with desperate intensity. Were others doing the same?

The blackness was throbbing like bees and reaching onwards and upwards into nothingness. Or else Jon was seeing from his cliff-top matters hidden from here by the lie of the land. Or cloud like a curtain had dropped between earth and sky. Or the Heavens were full of smoke. Or the warning was a false alarm.

Oh, how shocking a false alarm would be.

People in dread dragged themselves and their children down to the sand to meet the incomprehensible Maker of the World, but met confusion and noise, their children fractious and bewildered, not liking this sudden change in their lovely South Sea island.

Old man Everard, arriving at the head of his household, strode out of the palms. No one could see him but everyone knew he was there. At full voice he announced, 'For as the lightning cometh out of the east, and shineth even unto the west, so shall His coming be.'

For once Everard was wrong. It was as black as a tunnel. The people did not echo him. There were no hallelujahs.

The people you could see were but presences. You knew they were people because they were different from trees.

A woman brushed by. 'Where's Kerry? Kerry? Kerry?'

The school bell rang intermittently as if primed by nervous impulses of its own. Who, for pity's sake, could be left in bed?

The drum missed a beat. It missed another. And quietness dropped out of the sky. Your substance rose up to meet the sound, but met nothing. For a few moments you felt sick and deprived, but then in the humming silence an almost unbearable stress fell away, and from Jessie and Phoebe escaped part of the universal sigh. For a few cramped seconds every living thing with roots in the earth shared the relief, shared the release, until the silence and darkness and mystery of the sky became a question that was larger, infinitely larger than any other part of life.

'What is it? What's the boy seen?'

'Brigadier!'

The Brigadier remained as silent as the skies; the

throbbing skies; the skies that were without moon or stars; the skies that held and hid the mystery, and were featureless but *alive*.

The stillness became alarming for in some strange way it was filled with motion and sound and an overbearing presence. Small children didn't cry. Voices, murmuring, became lower and fewer.

Jessie and Phoebe clutched tighter through their hands.

The humming of the silence had edges like knives.

The air was super-charged, *alive*.

The drum boomed once, as if far away, as if stifled. None would have heard it if the silence had not come down.

It boomed again, clearer and stronger. Had there been a three-second pause?

Again it boomed – and seconds lay between. Again it boomed. And again. And the dread three seconds lay between.

A voice rose up in anger, in outrage. 'The lights! The lights in camp! Put out the lights!'

Beyond the coconut grove, beyond the foreshore, was there a hut not showing its light? It was like a street glittering at night. Every door left open. Every candle left alight. What a target. What a slaughter.

'The lights! Out! Out!'

Every three seconds the drum boomed.

'*Brigadier!*'

Old man Everard projected his voice. 'Fear not, my brethren. He that shall endure unto the end, the same shall be saved.'

'You'd better tell that to the Japanese!'

You had nothing to fight with. No shield. No weapon. You'd come empty-handed. You were betrayed.

The Japanese.

You wanted to run north, south, east, west. You wanted to remove yourself, divide yourself, become unfindable like pieces thrown into dark waters.

'Where's my Kerry? Answer me!'

'I wish we had our mum,' Phoebe said.

The drum boomed in the booming of the surf, in the booming of your head and in the booming of your blood.

'The guns are in camp,' Hancock bellowed. 'What's that boy done? We're in the wrong place.'

'Jon, what've you done?'

'What's the Brigadier's plan? Where is the man?'

The drum was booming still.

A shape near the blackness of the sea, a man with small children, started shouting and shrieking and shaking his fists. 'Bloody hell. Bloody hell.'

Spiderlike, a woman leapt upon him. '*Darling, no. Darling, please.*'

It could have been anyone they knew.

She struggled with him and clung to him while Everard from a distance had his say about the imminent presence of God.

'Attention! Attention!'

They were coming in company, Hawkins and Cunningham, the two camp guards with them, four men running erratically through the grove, and the trunks of the trees were an obstacle course and candlelight flickered beyond them like signals coded for the end of the world.

'Attention. Attention.'

The drum-beat fell silent as if by the command, and it was Cunningham with the megaphone. 'We can't read the signal any more than you can. Perhaps the sentry isn't sure. Perhaps he's done his best. Something must be wrong, we know.'

'*Where's the Brigadier?*'

'The Brigadier's ill.'

Hawkins yelled, 'Ill be damned. He's drunk.'

'Never, never,' shouted Chambers.

'Drunk,' yelled Hawkins. 'Blind, stupid, disgusting drunk.'

'Not true. Not true.' There was no mistaking Dr Weatheral's accent or anger. 'He hasn't slept for months. He's not drunk. I gave him pills.'

'*You gave him what?*'

'I'm his doctor. He's my patient. I gave him sleeping

136

pills. That, sir, is the end of it! If you'd been awake for a year, I'd have given them to you, too!'

'*You gave pills to the Brigadier. That, sir, is like hitting the driver on the head. And if he's your patient, why is he back there unattended while you are here?*'

Lights were bursting into brilliance far above; lights with haloes, like lights in fog. Dozens, dozens of lights were following one upon the other, coming down, and the humming in the air, the humming in the stillness, had little to do with God.

'Parachute flares! Air raid! Take cover!'

Take cover under a palm tree? Take cover on the open beach? Take cover while lights from which your eyes flinched fell from Heaven? Were you to burrow into the sand? Were you to leap into the sea and allow the dark ocean to close over your head?

You could hear the engines of aeroplanes. You could hear whistling sounds. Engines and whistlings became louder, became nearer, began to sound like screams.

Jessie and Phoebe ran like mad people along the curve of the beach. Perhaps they were running before the others because of total understanding, because they knew of somewhere to run.

People ran many different ways, dragging their children, dragging each other.

You had to do something, even if you didn't know what.

Then the bombs burst and who could believe that the wonderful vision of S.W.O.R.D. should die by the violent actions of men?

Thirty-One

(February 16, 1942)

They ran. They ran. They ran. Jessie and Phoebe. They ran along the beach towards the foot of the cliff. But the world was full of awful light and awful sound and awful pressures like sweeping flat-handed blows from giants as big as gods, and the only place to go was into the sand, into the sand, throwing themselves down as if diving into pools, while their ears split and their spirits reeled and their flesh shrank in horror from the tearing world.

They burrowed into the sand, wriggled into it, writhed into it, and somehow found the other's hand to hold. The only way to live or die was together.

Jon saw flares of white fire falling from Heaven making light of the night, light of the waves, light of the sands of the shore, light of the dark carpet of shiny palms, light even of the flashes and splashes of bursting bombs.

It was like the painting of a battle, a great painting, exploding from the canvas into real fire, catching Jon between amazement and shock, for below the levels of logic he had believed the Brigadier. He had expected God to come.

The irony of the fires that dropped from above was an irony of disillusionment. The heroes were the heroes of Japan, not the heroes of God.

Were the fires here the same as the fires on the horizon far off? Fires from Japan falling over some other island far off? It was a war like everyone else's war; not like God's glorious coming to say 'Enough!'

138

The Brigadier's heart would break. He'd cry out, 'This can't be what you meant for your people. It's not what you promised your people.'

Oh, all the poor people. Where were his mother and father and brother? Scattering like rabbits in terror? All the poor people; where were they to go?

Oh, Kerry, where are you while the bombs come down? If they kill you, I'll die.

Oh, Jessie and Phoebe; I'm sorry you're in it. I'm sorry, sorry.

Can you tell us, Brigadier, where we hide when the bombs come down? We can't hold them back by yelling and shouting. We can't step aside or run away, for they fall where they're going to fall and we're underneath them or we're not.

Down they come; down; for that is Nature's Law.

Shouldn't we have dug some trenches? Didn't we have time?

All the poor people with nowhere to go.

Jon sat cross-legged in the booth, with the thatch of palm leaves above him to keep off the sun and the rain, and fires below spread among the palm trees where the huts were, and fires ran like streams through the vegetable gardens and burned in flaring puddles on the sands and across the face of the cliff.

Everywhere, everywhere, bombs that made fire.

Jon couldn't bear it.

A step from the drum Hogan dropped like a log to his chest, jarring every bone and yet managing to save his glasses from collision with the earth. An afterthought hit him on the way down: '*Gawd. Me glasses!*' Then he struck and crunched the wind out of himself and gasped, 'I've busted me jaw. I've smashed me ribs.'

He spat out chips of teeth.

'Oh, hell!'

Bombs were bursting. Real bombs.

'Oh, hell, hell, hell.'

He threw his hands across the back of his neck and

shielded his eyes with his raised forearm. He'd give the arm to anyone. 'Take it.' As long as they left him his glasses and the rest of his teeth.

Gawd. Blood everywhere. Fancy breaking me teeth.

Fancy wearing me glasses with bombs going off. How not to do it, mate, in one lesson, but where do you put 'em if you don't hang them on your head? Put them anywhere else and who'll find them when the heat goes off?

Off the edge of the cliff he'd go, groping for his glasses as he plunged into the depths, tumbling over and over, down and down. Break more than a few teeth then. Smash more than his glasses. So he tried to sink into the ground right where he was, to soak into it like soup, but lay stranded on the hard surface, stark, stranded, stranded, like a wreck on rock, while the earth shook and wailed under him as if recoiling from each blast, as if grunting to each impact or crying out. Perhaps, like Hogan, the Earth had nerve ends. Perhaps, like Hogan, it felt pain and alarm and shock and yelled like hell when it got hurt.

How many aircraft had he seen in his vision of the world beyond the water? How many of them chock full of bombs? How many bombs? How many yet to face?

'Hell,' Hogan shouted, directly into the dirt. 'What a mess. Did it have to turn out like this? A mess. A mess. Fancy getting bombed. Come on, Heroes. Shake a leg. Come on in with your swords of light, but I always feared the Brigadier would only half be right. All the Sundays. Listening to thirty-eight thousand lectures to get the message that it's all for nix. Sitting up here for seven solid months toasting to a crisp.

'Hell,' yelled Hogan, and counted sixty-four distinct bomb-bursts, and lost count, and heard lumps of metal as big as fists whining, zinging, and the drum above his head thudding from shrapnel strikes while the earth shook and shrieked.

'Do we blame Jon for the Japs,' Hogan said into the dirt, 'what difference could he have made, mate, awake or asleep? Could he have stopped them with his binoculars? Could he aim his binoculars? Could he aim his binoculars

140

and go bang-bang? All those ships. All those aeroplanes
with their little windows on top and their bellies full of
bombs and no air raid shelter to keep the bombs off.

'They're dropping bombs on me, those beggars are. A
real nasty-minded personal attack, and I wouldn't know
'em from Adam if I bumped into them in the street. Gawd,
I wish I was with Auntie Sophie at Quambertook.

'Up I sat in that bed, you know, electric as a live wire,
and never felt like it before in me life. Off I flew with wings
on me feet. So is God a Jap? How'd that be for a shock?'

The air broke, the earth shook, there were flashes outside
as of lightning storms, and Kerry was called back from her
dream to find herself standing stiffly beside the Brigadier's bunk, as if transported there without notice from
some other place. In her stomach was a knot like a knuckle
of iron, and she felt cold, yet hot, and nerves like needles
ran wildly through her flesh. The world outside the bolted
door, outside the walls of bamboo and the roof of thatch,
made sounds and movements like typhoons and earth-
quakes, shocking her with the sounds, buffeting her with
the pressures, searing her with the fumes and smells of
sulphur and acid and phosphorus and smoke.

Was this the coming of God and his Heroes of Light?
God with aeroplane engines? God with high explosives to
annoint His people?

Would God descend upon S.W.O.R.D. with fire and
smoke?

'Sir', Kerry said, raising her voice until it was shrill and
toneless, 'this can't be God. You've got to wake up.'

But how could he have heard her? She barely heard
herself.

'It's a Japanese attack,' she shouted. 'We'll be killed if
you don't wake up.'

She fell upon him and pummelled him and shouted
again, 'Wake up.'

He moved under her as if turning in sleep, and with
desperate force she propelled him on through the turn and
thudded him over the edge of his bunk into the mat – and

never even wondered where she found the strength to move him or the agility to avoid him in the fiery gloom as he fell.

She went on punching at him, slapping at him, shouting at him, until two enormously strong arms silenced her with a bear hug.

'Kerry?' His voice was thick, slow and hard against her.

'Yes,' she shrilled, and struggled to break his grasp, appalled by his strength.

'Japanese?'

'Yes. Yes.'

'*Lie still*!' The sudden command sounded like her man, like her own Brigadier, yet she knew he wasn't in control or he'd not crush her so much. She felt like nothing, like an insect in a clenched fist.

'*Face down, Kerry*!'

His meaning was clear when he suddenly let her go and dragged the straw mattress from his bunk. She felt it flop over her from head to foot, as if to smother her, and felt the pressure of his great weight bear across the mattress like a shield against the sky. She could barely move or breathe for the weight of it, but she struggled no more, just prayed for the bombs to stop.

His weight left her as suddenly as it had come upon her. The mattress was pitched aside.

'Up,' he said.

He plucked her to her feet, and fire, real fire, was falling in showers from the thatch, falling about them both.

'Out,' he said, and lurched with her to the door, knocking from the table the oil lamp, the ink well, the brandy bottle, and the Doomsday Book. Oil from the lamp became fire, brandy from the bottle became fire, but Kerry swept up the Doomsday Book into her left hand.

The Brigadier opened the door and took her out into the lane, two or three strong strides, then stopped and raised his free arm to protect her.

The lane was a place of fire, smoke, flaring trees, molten huts, and winds which gusted masses of fire and blasts of heat, as if opposing ranks of fire swayed and billowed majestically to instructions.

There were no people and no traces of people.

Fire was bursting free on all sides, beyond the first lane, and the second lane, and farther yet, out where the gardens were and goats and Rhode Island Reds were and nameless creatures ran in circles as if lost.

There seemed to be nothing but fire and nowhere to go where fire was not.

'Now we die,' Kerry said to herself and held hard to her Brigadier by the hand.

'God be with you, Kerry,' he said, and ran with her as if into the flames.

Suddenly, she seemed to be running alone but had not felt his hand go, was sure she held his hand still, yet was sure she must be dead, though running still, drawing breaths as hot as the fire, her flesh burning like the fire, and she was sure it was her spirit only that fled.

Then, by surprise, she was in a cool place.

Thirty-Two

(February 16, 1942)

Apparently Kerry was wading in a sea of strong currents and shifting sand which surged about her, dragging her, pulling her, extinguishing the smouldering fabrics that clothed her, easing her burns and cooling her flesh, but continuing to drag her out deeper yet, carrying her from her feet into depths of uncertainty where she might or might not be able to stay afloat.

Was this the real sea of the real world of Tangu Tangu, or a condition of judgement in some other place? It looked real enough and felt real enough and its crests glowed with firelight. So she hadn't been lifted to the safe place; she was neither spirit nor ghost; just Kerry Coventry Shuffle, human survivor, born March 12, 1925, the same.

The same and alone.

Her right hand was empty and ached from its emptiness. He had taken her hand protectively – as he had burst from the stupor of his sleep – and she still could feel his huge strength and the purpose of his touch.

'God be with you, Kerry,' he had said; his last words on Earth; a blessing, not a curse; but the physical touch that had taken her through fire was as human as death and quite gone from her, the fire had taken it from her, and she had not felt the break. It was a break that left her with a wound bigger than life. All she had of him was his heavy, heavy book, held aloft.

Would she be swept out to sea now, to vanish, to drown, to be drawn down by creatures of the deep? It didn't matter, but she hoped it wouldn't hurt.

She dropped her feet as if to touch for the bottom and was well out of depth, and the sea was deepening farther, was swelling. It had the *feel* of increasing depth. But it might have been bearing her again like debris to the shore instead of carrying her farther out. It dumped her, thumped her, and withdrew, sweeping, dragging, half-covering her in wet soft sinking sliding sand, out of which she crawled with difficulty and numbness.

There she sprawled and said into the sand, 'Why have you left me alone?' She was not able to cry. She felt little but the immensity of the gulf between the living and the dead, and the awful loneliness that came suddenly upon her, the insecurity of it and the panic of it. Yet in the real world bombs were not bursting any more and the aeroplanes were silent, leaving only the heat and fumes and shock of their coming and going.

'Why have you left me living,' she said into the sand, 'but taken life away from me?'

Something touched Kerry, a human touch, that rolled her over with unusual care, as if her body might disintegrate or was already dead. It was not the touch of her Brigadier, or of her mother either.

'Is she alive?' someone said. 'How'd she get here?'

The person kneeling at her side worked an arm under her shoulders and sat her up.

'It's good to find you, Kerry. Really good.'

Kerry shook her head.

'Are you able to walk? I mean, right now.'

'He's dead,' Kerry said.

'What's that she's got? The Doomsday Book. Where'd you get it?'

'Who's dead, Kerry?'

'He was with me. We were together.'

'I think she means the Brigadier. Didn't they say he was asleep?'

'Look, Kerry, it's dangerous being here. We've got to move. We've got to get to the other side of the island and real quickly. We've got to get off this place or we're dead

145

ducks, sure as eggs, sure as eggs.'

'Where's my mother?' Kerry said, peering at Jessie and Phoebe in the lowering glow.

'Come on. It's going to be bad for us if we're seen. There's a warship out there. We're dead lucky the dinghy's on the other side. We'd never get it away from here.'

'Where's everyone?' Kerry said.

'There's us. The three of us. There's no one else.'

Kerry opened her right arm in a gesture that took in all of Tangu Tangu – the visible and devastated, and the distant and not seen. 'Where's everyone?'

'There's us,' Jessie wailed. 'The three of us. Don't you hear? Lordy!'

Phoebe thrust out a determined leg and wrenched Kerry to her feet. 'Now run, sister. You listen to me. You make the effort. We don't want to die even if you do.'

Kerry suddenly resented them. They were bullies. Two bullies. Each an image of the other. They were dragging her.

'What's the use of going anywhere?' she shrieked. 'We can't sail a dinghy. Sail it out to sea. Sail it where?'

They went on dragging her and her legs moved with limp drawn-out strides that were given stretch because they lifted her, half-carried her, even though she wished only to collapse and forget she'd been born.

'What are we doing?' she yelled, for they seemed to be going nowhere except sideways, backwards, one way, another way, without direction. It was pointless. Who cared what happened now? The smoking surface was strewn with lumps of earth and rock and torn and up-ended roots and nameless burning obstacles. Where were the people? It was a wasteland. Uninhabited. No one ran before them or beside them. No one rose up near them through the smoke. How could it be that no one else was going their way?

The thought was too awful to admit, but it pressed upon her and pressed upon her. Everyone was dead. Her life was dead. S.W.O.R.D. was dead. Of all those lovely people only these clod-hoppers were left.

It looked like the abomination of desolation at the end of the world. It *was* the end of the world.

'Tell me where everyone is?' she shrieked.

They shouted back as with one voice. *Shut-up. Save your breath. Run and don't ask stupid questions.*

She found herself trying to run, trying like a bone-weary, backbroken, bullied beast, but wished only to fall and go where her Brigadier had gone, before he'd gone too far to be found. This uninhabited world of Tangu Tangu was finished. This nether world was the awful dream from which she had to wake.

They'd stopped. If they'd lost their way, serve them right! Kerry drooped between them, coughing. Around them was a glowing maze, grey with smoke haze and the approach of dawn. It should have been the vegetable and fruit gardens. Kerry felt utterly lost in spirit, utterly fatigued in body, and wanted to lie down, but hot ashes were ankle deep and her feet felt as if they must surely ignite.

All the landmarks had changed. Huge rough holes and scarred and displaced trees were rearing from areas of ground-smoke through which one would be mad to pass. Smells came in waves like gunpowder or fungus or roasting grain; smells and vapours that made their eyes stream and their nerves flinch. Over farther where the hut lanes used to be, heaps of coals glowed with heat and light and were scattered by winds that turned them into fiery pillars collapsing in showers of sparks like rain.

'No good this way,' Phoebe cried. 'We can't get through. No good. No good. Don't know where we're going to get through. Do you think the whole world's like it?'

'Who'd ever have imagined it,' wailed Jessie.

'We can't get anywhere. Only the cave. If we swim.'

'All right. Let's swim.'

They dragged Kerry back again, this way, that way, as if all directions were wrong directions, round the mounds and craters and active fires, and came back onto the pale beach, upwind of the worst of the heat.

They could barely breathe for the stress of smoke and exertion, for the fright, for the certainty of drowning in that sea.

The pale beach; there it lay in the half light like a dirty ribbon or a littered road. In the west the burning forest shot clouds of sparks and masses of smoke to an enormous height, so high that the upper reaches caught the light of the sun not yet up. In the east the dark cliff smouldered as if lava seared its surface and in the north two ships like shadows stood offshore. Even as Jessie gasped out what Phoebe saw, 'Two ships, not one,' there were gashes of red and yellow flame almost simultaneously from both vessels, fore and aft.

They had never seen the like of it, but knew what it was about.

There was time only to plunge into the sand, Kerry plunging with them, caught in the same reflex of horror, as if this were the ultimate end of life.

They felt the shells strike the ground, felt earth and rock shudder, and with the shock came a savage stinging of sand, of sharpness, of edges blasting across them.

Thirty-Three

(February 16, 1942)

Jon on the cliff-top was like a minor god on a cloud, set above a world he had meddled with, a world he had ruined. Oh, the remorse he felt and the dread for the lives of others. Oh, the fright that grew inside him as if to burst, for he was but a spectator, helpless, and his shocked senses were rushing towards peaks too great to bear. The peaks drove him out of the world. They placed him in darkness somewhere else.

It was as if he actually knew the ruined world lay behind him, elsewhere. It was as if he was aware of it for a period long enough for the ruined world to disappear. Now, if he reached out, he'd find a new door and light of a new kind would break upon him. Perhaps a searing light of judgement. Perhaps the gentle light of forgiveness. But he could not extend his hand. He tried, he strove, but went on hearing only the long quietness of being outside, and seeing only its blackness, and feeling only its density about him like bonds binding him hand and foot.

The blackness then began to turn grey, began to make sounds, began to lose its density, causing him to fall away from the unreachable door until it was no longer there. Then he saw again and heard again the ruined world of pain. It burned and S.W.O.R.D. burned with it. And Jon was face to face with the disaster that the Brigadier's vision of fire was the prophetic one, that the vision of S.W.O.R.D.'s deliverance was wrong, that the evil in the world was not burning, that the splendid vision of saving the world was a mirage. And death was the cost.

It seemed so unfair.

A bewildered cry arose in him. 'The Bijou was incredible, marvellous, miraculous. How can it be a lie?'

He was bleeding. There were warm, sticky places. He didn't care. There were hot spots where he hurt. He didn't care. His face stung shockingly. He didn't care. He had half-fallen against a corner post, his legs absurdly crossed, as if propped on a bed of nails for passers-by to take shots at. They'd been scoring hits.

The passers-by were Japanese in aeroplanes, were Japanese in ships, but closer yet was Hogan, yellow in the yellow light, with fire glints in his eyes and blood on his mouth, hand raised to strike Jon on the cheek.

'Jon. Jon. Jon. Jon.'

The island burned as if fuelled from within. A million burning fragments fell to the sea. Smoke, red, dark and raw, boiled to high Heaven. Sparks like flecks of tinsel, lay upon his clothes.

'Jon!'

'Yes.'

'Come on.'

Hogan had grown.

'We're useless here,' Hogan said. 'We'll have to break orders. Our place is down there.'

He was absolutely right, urgently right, so right that Jon was ashamed he had not thought of it long before. He lurched to his feet striking the cross bar of the booth a heavy blow with the back of his neck, but barely feeling the hurt.

'The aeroplanes'll come again,' Hogan said, 'or the ships'll fire their guns.'

Yes, thought Jon. Of course, of course. Oh, dear Kerry and dear people.

They launched themselves onto the path worn by their many comings and goings. They ran, leapt, floundered, scrambled.

Imagine, thought Jon, *this* fellow is my companion for the end of the world.

The stubble of the cliff-face smouldered where fire had

burnt among the boulders. Earth and stones steamed. Air swirled hot, luminous and acrid and stung their throats and lungs.

'Our hut's gone.'

Jurgen's burnt, thought Jon. Oh, damn.

My stamps, thought Hogan. How many years? My Doomsday Book. Here I go starting an oral tradition. Dear grandchildren; in the beginning God. And in the end the same.

Explosions were happening not far away. Drums of lighting kerosene? Drums of fuel? No.

Hogan said, 'Now they're bombarding us.'

'Everything's gone, Hogan.' A long wail escaped from Jon. His family. All the families. His beautiful Kerry.

'Next there'll be hundreds of soldiers,' Hogan said.

They floundered away through glowing smoke, hopping through blistering ashes. It was an unrecognizable place, yet here the Brigadier used to ride his bike back and forth.

'Head for the beach,' Hogan said. Jon said it, too.

Shell-bursts, as if patterned like a fan, erupted through areas already aflame, all around, appearing to come from the cliff-top and the shoreline, from the gardens and hut lanes, and from where the glades would lie between. What difference did it make, if you ran like a rabbit or dug a hole? What difference whether you were here or there? The shells would miss or cut you down, Lady Luck the chooser.

Which way the beach? How did you see with smarting, streaming eyes? How did you not fry by inches from the feet up? How did you not choke for want of a breath of something clean?

Hundreds of soldiers, Hogan thought. My gawd.

Hundreds of soldiers, Jon thought, not thinking in a straight line, thinking in flashes. All those poor women. All the poor children.

Hundreds of soldiers coming with bayonets on their rifles, and grenades and sub-machine guns. Like locusts. Like destroyers. Like something unimaginable. They'll come with the daylight, after the bombs stop, after the shells stop.

Not much time, Hogan thought. Not much time to sunrise. Where's the beach? Not much time to get there. Not much time to live or die. It's a long way back to King Edward Street. Oh hell. And dead lies the world.

It's got to happen soon, thought Jon. Sun-up, or cinders. Where's this beach? Everybody waiting there in a huddle for the massacre? Or everyone swimming out to sea – men, women, children, infants – through ranks of landing craft filled with soldiers? What a hope.

Where's the beach? God knows. We've turned too many ways.

Who'll survive this? Hogan thought. Everything plastered with bombs, plastered with incendiaries, everything whistling with shell fragments, take your leg off, take your head off, everything blown to burning bits. Can't breathe for burning bits. How these bloody bombs burn. I don't fancy your chances, Mum, and that's tough. But look at us. Maybe you're not dead either. People'll be injured though. Lying injured everywhere. Lying dead. I hope we've still got a doctor and a nurse. What do you do with people that are really hurt? I should have done First Aid when I had the chance. No people anywhere, anywhere. Shouldn't we be seeing people everywhere through here, lying down dead or injured or running alive?

There was the beach, the beautiful beach, there was the sea, and an uncertain distance away, in the fire-glow, in the gunflashes, objects lay on the sand. Were they blasted trees? The palms at the shore-line were snapped like sticks.

Thirty-Four

(February 16, 1942)

Ships were offshore, but they barely saw them. They knew numbers of small boats were there also, though they were not aware of incoming movement. Boats were roped in lines, in lanes, like beads on strings. Dozens of boats filled with soldiers were riding on the dark waves, rising and falling. Shells were whining overhead and striking inland. These matters Jon and Hogan knew but did not precisely observe.

Both pointed along the beach. 'There!' And both felt sick and thought of everyone they loved and everyone they knew. It was a fall into great depths. How could they be bits of trees? They were people. They were family. They were S.W.O.R.D.

Each grasped the other by an arm and communicated with sympathy for the first time in their lives.

At first the bodies seemed but a touch away. The distance stretched as they ran. They were in dread of what they must find, but ran to find it, bent low, limbs growing heavier, heavier. The distance stretched farther, farther, through deep soft ridges where bomb craters or shell holes scored the sand.

There the bodies were overlaid as if sand and ash had swept across them or they'd burrowed like beetles. The objects that looked like bits of trees truly were bits of trees. Three bodies, and they'd reckoned on a score.

Oh, the poor girls. You loved each one. Jon fell beside Kerry and touched her sacred body while his spirit soared.

'Thank you,' he said, with eyes clamped closed, because he felt the breath of life there and the nerve of it.

'This is the one I love,' he said. 'I'll die for her.'

In one hand she clutched a book that Jon could not take from her. He recognized it and said, 'We all love the Brigadier. There's nothing strange about that.' Strength grew in him as he knelt there, enough to bear her weight and to rise with it.

Hogan was in another dimension, yelling as if from rage. 'Phoebe, Jessie, get up for gawd's sake. You're not dead yet.'

Jessie jolted to her knees and grasped at Phoebe's hand, a hand that moved limply without a will of its own. But each girl could have been the other, for all that Hogan knew or saw.

'She's not moving,' Jessie shrieked, dragging on her sister by the arm. 'You must get up, you must. Are you dead? Is she dead? She's dead. Who's that there? Is she dead?'

'*It's Hogan.*'

'If Phoebe's dead I'll kill myself right now. Right now I'll run into the sea.'

Hogan hit her.

Jon lurched off among the blasted trees, Kerry over his back. Timbers still cracked and fell. Sparks still showered. Smoke curled, drifted, almost like a fog.

'Take care of us please,' he said to God, then added, 'but I wonder if you have a mind to, from the look of things round here.'

He wished he could have carried Kerry in his arms, could have seen her, could have held her close, could have comforted her for his own sake as well as hers, but he didn't have the strength for that. He'd find a place somewhere instead, quickly, quickly, and lean her head against him until the Japanese came with their guns.

Hogan yelled at Jessie. 'Soldiers, do you hear? We've got to warn people. We've got to find people. We've got to get out of here. Take your sister's feet, you stupid lump.'

The sun was up.

154

Hell, it was up, suddenly adding fire to fire, and everything was red with the glow. Nowhere to hide now, except in the smoke, except among the flames.

'We looked everywhere,' Jessie cried. 'There's only us. *Where's Kerry?*'

'She's *gone* with Jon. Grab her feet, will you! Gawd, you're dumb!'

'Is Jon alive? Is that what you say?'

'Lady, he's not carryin' Kerry on his back because he's dead. Take her feet!'

'Jon's alive,' Jessie cried, 'and Phoebe's dead. She's the strong one. I'll die.' But she took Phoebe's feet, weeping and staggering, and bore her away with Hogan, struggling up through the sand into the blasted, blackened foreshore.

'She's so damn' heavy,' Hogan groaned. 'Heavy enough to be dead. We'll not be getting her far. We'll not be getting anywhere, I reckon. Where's bloody Jon?'

If only this oaf could be Jon, thought Jessie. Jon's beautiful. Jon'd never hit me. Jon'd understand. But Jon's gone with her and she doesn't give a fig for him. You're like lead, Phoeb. Don't be dead or I'll die. You're so heavy, Phoeb. It's awful everyone being dead. All the people except us and Jon and her. I don't think I can carry you another yard.

Hogan thought, where am I going, where is there to go? Don't these girls know the island better than anyone?

Phoebe slid from Jessie's numbed grasp and she wept from the hopelessness.

Hogan said, 'One more try. Get her up and over my shoulders. If Jon can carry Kerry, so can I. Help me, Jessie.'

'She's dead. Leave us to die.'

'She'll be dead, I'm telling you, if you don't get her over my shoulders. Try!'

Jessie heard, but didn't hear. Heard *try*. Heard *shoulders*. And the effort wrenched her to her heart and bones, but there was Hogan, trying to anchor his feet, swaying, tottering, shrieking, 'Keep her there. Hold her there.

Steady me. Oh my gawd. Now a hiding place. Quickly. Where can we go?'

'We've tried. We've done all that,' Jessie wailed. 'You can't get to anywhere. Everything's too far away.'

'Rubbish,' shrieked Hogan. 'The hiding place where the people are. Where the Brigadier is. You mapped the island. You must know.'

'There aren't any people,' Jessie cried. 'I keep saying.'

'Of course there are people or there'd be bodies lyin' everywhere. Why aren't you with them? Why are you alone?'

Jessie sat on the ground. She couldn't cope with his cruelty or stupidity.

'Get up, for gawd's sake,' shrieked Hogan, black sweat pouring into his eyes, his glasses like dirty windows. 'Do you get the message! The Japanese! They'll mince you, kid!'

'There's the cave under the cliff,' Jessie said in a flat voice, 'but it's dangerous.'

'What cave, for gawd's sake?'

'You get to it along the beach.'

'Oh marvellous,' said Hogan. 'Just what we need. A nice run along the sand in clear sight of their guns.'

'You could go along here,' Jessie said, 'if you want to. We found hundreds of bones in that cave. Skulls and all. A real shock. But you've got to swim to get in. So how'd they have got the little ones in there? And the old ones? And would they have run over the top of us on the way?'

'You've got to face it, kid. Do you see the bodies? Broad daylight and no bodies. The people are somewhere safe.'

'There's nowhere safe in miles.'

'Rubbish,' shrieked Hogan. 'We'd be tripping over corpses. Let's get to the cave.'

'They won't be there.'

'Oh my gawd. Do you take me or do I drop your sister on her head? Give us a break, kid. Get moving!'

'If the tide's in, you'll drown getting into it.'

'Okay, we'll drown. Gawd, I wish I could see for meself. Can't see a damn thing. I'll be wobbling here screaming me head off when the Japs come ashore.'

'I want to die,' Jessie said, but she got up and made her way a step or two ahead. It was possible now. Fires were burning farther off. Now the fires were black or low, making smoke, or daylight diminished the glow.

'Don't miss Jon and Kerry! Keep your eyes peeled! He doesn't know where to go. He's never heard of the cave.'

'No one's heard of it,' Jessie said, 'except us and the Brigadier. That's why no one can be there. The Brigadier was asleep.'

'Don't be stupid,' shrieked Hogan, planting each foot as if a hammer drove it into the ground. These kids'll be the death of me and this one'll break my blinking back. If she's dead it's an awful lot of work for nothing. Then he thought of Carrie, his sister, aged nine, and choked up.

'I can't see Jon or Kerry,' Jessie said.

'You're not caring! You're not trying!'

'I am trying!'

'Well, where the hell is he?'

'The smoke's like a fog.'

'Well that makes two of us who can't see a damn thing.' Hogan was beginning to stagger. 'But the Japs wear glasses same as me. They're blind, same as me. Good luck to the beggars. I hope they fall down a hole. Jon! For gawd's sake, I bet you he's down a bomb hole!'

'Jon,' he shouted. 'Here we are. Give us a hoy.'

'Jon,' cried Jessie, though her voice would not have carried far.

There was no answering call, except gunfire from the sea and shells bursting a mile away.

'Oh, hell,' groaned Hogan, 'what a mess.'

Jon in his shell-hole guided Kerry until her head rested on his chest. He held her shoulders tightly, sometimes searching for her pulse with his finger-tips. He kissed her hair, but she didn't know and didn't object.

He spoke to her, without voice. 'This is what I've lived my life for. To hold you as close as this. I've never held a girl, never kissed a girl, never touched. You're the one. You're the last. If they want to hurt you, Kerry, they'll have to kill me first.'

Then he said a prayer.

'It looks like we've been wrong. That You never made the promise, or never made it to us. I'm sorry about that. I believed, earnestly believed, except on the bad days. Please take care of all the lovely people, wherever they are. Please forgive the Brigadier, because he believed what he said. Could he stand up as he did, and not believe? But it's true, like my Headmaster said; so many times it's happened; the prophets talking about the end of the world, but the world not ending. Talking about your coming back to clean things up, but your not coming. I wonder why? Where do we get the idea from, if it always comes to nothing? Please take care of Kerry, even if not of me. She's so beautiful. She's so good. I love her.'

Jon looked up, because someone was looking down.

Phoebe's weight was bearing Hogan down beyond endurance. 'I'm sorry, Jessie,' he said, and went suddenly onto one knee, and Phoebe spilled awkwardly to the ground. Then Jessie saw her sister's eyes looking back up at her.

'Phoebe,' Jessie shrieked. 'You're not dead. Oh, Phoeb. Oh, Phoeb. I thought you'd gone. I thought you'd left me on my own.'

Hogan stayed on one knee, hands braced to the ground, talking to himself while Jessie shrieked and wept. 'Not dead,' he groaned. 'Gawd, you wouldn't believe the state of my back. If she's not dead she can bloody walk the same as the rest of us.'

He thrust his hands into the small of his back and straightened up and at once saw Jon not far away. Or thought he saw Jon. 'Jon,' he yelled. But how would he be sure of anything through glasses so dirty it was like groping round in a coal mine? He rubbed them on the tail of his shirt and realized the world had gone quiet except for his own calls, 'Jon. Jon.'

There was no bombardment. There were no aircraft.

It wasn't Jon he saw when he replaced his glasses, but soldiers, soldiers, soldiers.

'Oh, hell,' said Hogan, and stepped in front of the girls.

Thirty-Five

(August 28, 1979)

Record of statement made on August 28, 1979, At Gifu, Japan, by Shoyo Maekawa, one-time senior intelligence officer, Headquarters, Fourteenth Division, Japanese Army, units of which invaded Tangu Tangu and islands of the Bismarck Archipelago on February 16, 1942.

Late in 1941 advice came to us from German intelligence that the Allied garrison on Tangu Tangu, code-named Sword, was commanded by a distinguished officer of the Australian Army, Brigadier General Palmer. Our own information confirmed that a garrison of some strength had been established there during July, 1941, and doubtless had received reinforcements. That an officer of Palmer's rank and experience should have been committed to an outpost, and that the garrison bore a provocative code-name, aroused our interest. The weight and severity of the attack on Tangu Tangu was the outcome.

The assault was an anti-climax. Our long-range bombing aircraft met no anti-aircraft fire and the landing met no resistance. Five prisoners only were taken, two males, three females, none of them of military age. The prisoners were removed to the flagship for medical treatment and interrogation. I was present during each of the several interrogations over the following five days.

Throughout prolonged questioning, individually and collectively, the prisoners asserted that Sword was not a military operation, that it was a religious community praying for peace, that the only weapons they had possessed were a few sporting rifles, and that the community had numbered precisely one hundred souls, men, women, and children. The general's diary, recovered from their possession, did not disprove this. A high degree of concern for the ninety-five missing persons was evident. All officers present during the interrogations were impressed by the dignity of the prisoners and their devotion to each other.

An intensive search of Tangu Tangu and surrounding seas was then undertaken. Further searches were made from time to time during the two years we occupied the island. I am able to state that no human remains attributable to our assault of February 16, 1942, were ever found.

The prisoners were brought to Japan in March, 1942. Interrogations continued. I was not present on these occasions. The prisoners are reported to have answered frankly all questions relating to their belief. It should be recorded that their calm demeanour and the evidence of our own investigations on Tangu Tangu aroused disquiet. Elements of that disquiet reached even to the Emperor's household and may have had influence upon subsequent events.

In May, 1942, the prisoners were removed to a safe place of confinement in Hokkaido. They survived the war and elected to live in Japan afterwards. One young woman of exceptional beauty entered a Buddhist convent in northern Honshu. I have no knowledge of the whereabouts of the others. I believe they are married.